P9-APT-074

"Susan? Is everything okay?"

No response.

Rand knocked on the bedroom door, but still couldn't raise anyone. Returning to the nursery, he tapped again, then opened the door a crack.

"Susan?" He peeked inside and saw her sitting in the rocker. Both Susan and Penny were sound asleep, though even in a deep sleep, Susan held her baby protectively against her.

Relieved, Rand shook his head. Poor girl. She was so exhausted, she probably could have gone to sleep standing up. He couldn't leave her that way. She hadn't even taken off her high heels.

He settled the baby into her bassinet, and she didn't stir at all. Rand watched her sleep. He would never admit it, but there was something about babies that got to him. He'd been in heaven this evening, taking over Penny's care. The baby girl was creeping under his skin.

And so was her mother.

Dear Reader,

Every month Harlequin American Romance brings you four powerful men, and four admirable women who know what they want—and go all out to get it. Check out this month's sparkling selection of love stories, which you won't be able to resist.

First, our AMERICAN BABY promotion continues with Kara Lennox's *Baby by the Book*. In this heartwarming story, a sexy bachelor comes to the rescue when a pretty single mother goes into labor. The more time he spends with mother and child, the more he finds himself wanting the role of dad....

Also available this month is *Between Honor and Duty* by Charlotte Maclay, the latest installment in her MEN OF STATION SIX series. Will a firefighter's determination to care for his friend's widow and adorable brood spark a vow to love, honor and cherish? Next, JUST FOR KIDS, Mary Anne Wilson's miniseries continues with an office romance between *The C.E.O. & the Secret Heiress*. And in *Born of the Bluegrass* by Darlene Scalera, a woman is reunited with the man she never stopped loving—the father of her secret child.

Enjoy this month's offerings, and be sure to return each and every month to Harlequin American Romance!

Wishing you happy reading,

Melissa Jeglinski
Associate Senior Editor
Harlequin American Romance

BABY BY THE BOOK
Kara Lennox

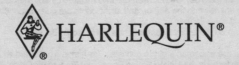

HARLEQUIN®

TORONTO • NEW YORK • LONDON
AMSTERDAM • PARIS • SYDNEY • HAMBURG
STOCKHOLM • ATHENS • TOKYO • MILAN • MADRID
PRAGUE • WARSAW • BUDAPEST • AUCKLAND

If you purchased this book without a cover you should be aware
that this book is stolen property. It was reported as "unsold and
destroyed" to the publisher, and neither the author nor the
publisher has received any payment for this "stripped book."

ISBN 0-373-16893-4

BABY BY THE BOOK

Copyright © 2001 by Karen Leabo.

All rights reserved. Except for use in any review, the reproduction or
utilization of this work in whole or in part in any form by any electronic,
mechanical or other means, now known or hereafter invented, including
xerography, photocopying and recording, or in any information storage
or retrieval system, is forbidden without the written permission of the
publisher, Harlequin Enterprises Limited, 225 Duncan Mill Road,
Don Mills, Ontario, Canada M3B 3K9.

All characters in this book have no existence outside the imagination of
the author and have no relation whatsoever to anyone bearing the same
name or names. They are not even distantly inspired by any individual
known or unknown to the author, and all incidents are pure invention.

This edition published by arrangement with Harlequin Books S.A.

® and TM are trademarks of the publisher. Trademarks indicated with
® are registered in the United States Patent and Trademark Office, the
Canadian Trade Marks Office and in other countries.

Visit us at www.eHarlequin.com

Printed in U.S.A.

ABOUT THE AUTHOR

Texas native Kara Lennox has been an art director, typesetter, advertising copy writer, textbook editor and reporter. She's worked in a boutique, a health club and has conducted telephone surveys. She's been an antiques dealer and briefly ran a clipping service. But no work has made her happier than writing romance novels.

When Kara isn't writing, she indulges in an ever-changing array of weird hobbies, from rock climbing to crystal digging. But her mind is never far from her stories. Just about anything can send her running to her computer to jot down a new idea for some future novel.

Books by Kara Lennox

HARLEQUIN AMERICAN ROMANCE

Don't miss any of our special offers. Write to us at the following address for information on our newest releases.

Harlequin Reader Service
U.S.: 3010 Walden Ave., P.O. Box 1325, Buffalo, NY 14269
Canadian: P.O. Box 609, Fort Erie, Ont. L2A 5X3

Dear Reader,

I've never had the privilege of giving birth to a child myself. Perhaps that is why I find the subjects of pregnancy, birth and babies so endlessly fascinating. So when my editor, Melissa Jeglinski, asked me if I had any "baby books" on the back burner, naturally I just happened to be noodling around with an idea.

I tried to make my heroine, Susan, as clueless as I would be with a first pregnancy—and as scared, excited and overwhelmed, not to mention worried about looking fat. Poor Susan really needed help getting the hang of diapers and bottles, which made it lots of fun to pair her with Rand, a confirmed bachelor who, nonetheless, knew everything about babies.

I can only imagine what it really feels like to bring a new life into the world, but writing it from Susan's viewpoint gives me a definite vicarious thrill. I hope you'll share it with me.

Best,

Kara Lennox

Chapter One

Rand Barclay wrestled with the baby crib, trying unsuccessfully to reduce it to two dimensions. It had been nice and flat when he'd brought it *down* from the attic two years ago, when his younger sister, Alicia, had come home from the hospital with Dougy. Now it refused to fold up.

He cursed the baby bed just as Clark Best walked into the room. Clark was his employee—estate manager, majordomo, butler, maid and cook rolled into one. The man was the epitome of efficiency, competence and hard work. He also happened to be Rand's best friend.

"Missing the little tyke already?" Clark asked, his eyes gleaming with mischief. He was up to something, but Rand had no idea what.

"The only thing I miss is my office," Rand growled. "And I'm taking it back. Now."

"Then let me do this." Clark bent down, flicked some invisible lever, and the crib folded right up. He smiled smugly, his blindingly white teeth flashing in stark contrast to his dark skin. "You want it in the attic?"

"Hell, no. Burn it. There will be no more babies in this house. Maybe I'll be able to get some work done around here."

Clark snorted. "We'll see about that." He left the room, carrying the crib effortlessly under one arm. At six-foot-three and two hundred and forty pounds, Clark made most things look effortless—including a cheese soufflé. An old buddy from high school, Clark was in his last year of cooking school at Savannah's Culinary Institute. He lived in one of Rand's many spare rooms and ate prodigious amounts of Rand's food in return for keeping the house running smoothly. Rand didn't know what he would do in a few months when Clark graduated, got real a job, and moved out.

Yes, he did know. Rand would be alone, just as he'd wanted to be since he'd bought this house after his first year at a successful medical practice. It had taken him the eight long years after that to get his three rambunctious younger sisters safely launched into the world.

Then there was his mother. Rand loved her dearly, but the obstinate Marjorie Barclay had clung to Rand and this house like a tic on a hound dog. He had used every persuasive trick he could think of to get her to move to South Carolina's most posh retirement village, where she could meet people her own age and develop some interests apart from her children. Fortunately, she'd adjusted quickly and now pretended the move had been all her idea.

Rand contemplated the stacks of research books that had grown like stalagmites around his office during the past six months. He'd been setting the stage for the massive task of writing his book—collecting papers and articles on rare skin diseases, tracking down subjects, accumulating stacks and stacks of statistics. But he had yet to commit a single word to paper.

Who could write with little kids underfoot and assorted females coming and going all the time, their high-pitched laughter and mindless chatter constantly in the background? One of his medical journals, he noticed, had a half-eaten lollipop stuck to it.

But that was all over now. As of today, he was embarking on a new life, one of total independence. For a while, at least, Rand Barclay was going to focus on Rand Barclay. He was going to do what he wanted, buy what he wanted, work, sleep and eat when he wanted—in blissful solitude.

And the first step was new bookshelves for his office—custom-made for his medical books and notes. Clark had already consulted a carpenter and negotiated a fee. Rand had signed off on the plans, which had arrived by messenger two days ago. Today the carpenter would start work.

Rand could hardly wait until the shelves were done. He could organize his research materials instead of pawing through unruly stacks every time he wanted to find a piece of information.

Clark came back into the room with a feather duster and went to work on Rand's desk without saying a word.

"So what time is the carpenter getting here?" Rand asked.

"Should be any time." Another mysterious smile. "But I still don't see why you chose *now* to have bookshelves built. You're supposed to finish your book...when?"

"End of next month," Rand said, trying to sound matter-of-fact. But whenever he thought about his deadline, his stomach swooped.

"And how much have you gotten written?"

Rand didn't answer.

"These bookshelves are just another excuse to procrastinate," Clark said. "You can give a man a license to practice medicine, set him up at a primo research lab, but deep down he's still a college kid, cramming for an exam at the last minute, finishing up a term paper at six in the morning—"

"I did not get through med school by procrastinating. And you have no idea what's involved in writing this textbook. It's not like writing a term paper. You have to lay the groundwork for something like this. If you don't make the proper preparations, the whole thing will get out of whack."

Clark rolled his eyes. "You can be the most pompous ass sometimes. And you don't call this out of whack?" He made a sweeping gesture, encompassing every last untidy pile.

"Yeah, yeah, put a sock in it."

Clark just smiled. They bantered like this all the time, and neither of them took offense. Clark had earned the right to insult Rand. He'd known Rand when he was "that no-good Barclay kid," knobby knees and ill-fitting shoes and clothes that never quite went together.

And yes, all right, Rand did procrastinate. He couldn't fool Clark, who'd been witness to Rand's time-management impairment since high school.

But the job always got done. And the treatise would get written, too, just as soon as he had proper book-shelves.

SUSAN KILGORE CLIMBED into her truck and cranked open the window before starting the engine. The weather was unseasonably warm for October, even in South Carolina. She checked the mirror, put her truck in gear and backed out of the driveway, waving to her landlady.

Harriet Regis was a dear, and Susan hated the fact that she had to move out of the Regises' attic apartment. But Mr. Regis was ill, and he needed a quiet tenant. Susan hadn't even waited for Harriet to bring it up. She'd already gone out and found another apartment. It wasn't as nice as this one, but it included a garage where she could set up her woodworking shop.

As she drove past a convenience store, Susan thought longingly of a cup of coffee. How long had it been since she'd had one?

No sense dwelling on all the things she couldn't or didn't have in her life right now, she lectured herself.

Better to focus on what she did have, which was her first significant paying job since her father's death more than a year ago.

She'd quickly discovered that potential customers had no faith in a woman's carpentry abilities. During the past few months, she'd scrounged up a little bit of work. She'd framed in a new door for her landlords, and she'd put new facings on the neighbor's kitchen cabinets. But the big jobs had eluded her. And, in truth, she hadn't tried as hard as she should have to get work.

But the little nest egg her ex-boyfriend had left her—purely out of guilt—was gone, along with almost all of her own savings. If she didn't revitalize the carpentry business immediately, she would have to get a nine-to-five job. And, let's face it, who was going to hire her at this point?

Thank goodness Clark Best had called, not realizing her father had passed on. She'd been completely honest with him, and then she'd had to grovel to get the job. But he'd given her a chance, bless his heart.

Now it was up to her to convince Dr. Rand Barclay that she could build him the most awesome shelving unit he'd ever seen—solid mahogany, brass hardware...

Oh, hell, who was she kidding? The minute he laid eyes on her, she would be out the door on her fanny.

CLARK WAS BUSY IN the kitchen when the doorbell rang, so Rand answered it himself. A tall woman with long, dark hair in a sleek ponytail stood on his front porch, looking around uncertainly. She carried a huge sketch pad in front of her, so he could see nothing of her figure, but from the shoulders up she was breathtaking.

She wasn't a classic beauty—her face was a bit too angular for that. But her skin was flawless, her lips pink and moist, and her eyes—they were hard to look away from. A startling blue, they seemed to hold emotional depths Rand could never fathom.

She blinked a couple of times at him. "Is this the Barclay residence?"

"Yes, ma'am. I'm Rand Barclay."

"Hello, Dr. Barclay. I'm Susan Kilgore." Clutching the sketch pad against her with one hand, she extended the other in an awkward handshake. Her hands were long, strong, and not very pretty, especially with those bitten nails. Yet Rand felt something odd when she touched him. He supposed it was because he wasn't used to a woman shaking hands like a man.

He waited for her to state her business. The silence stretched an uncomfortable length of time, and it seemed as if she expected to be invited in. Then he saw the truck in the driveway and the logo on the door: Kilgore Woodworking.

"Oh, the bookshelves," Rand finally said, feeling like an idiot. "Come right in." He looked past her out to the driveway, expecting her father or brother to appear, but apparently she was alone.

She stepped into the foyer and looked around.

"This is a fine old house," she said, almost wistfully. "I imagine it's been in your family forever."

"No. I've only had it eight years. Frankly, it's a bit of a pain. Always something going wrong."

Susan sighed. "Old houses just need a little more TLC—like old people."

"You have an old house then?"

"No, but someday…"

"The shelves go in here." He led her into his lair.

"Oh, my, yes," she said from behind him. "I see why Clark called."

Rand studied his office, trying to see it with her eyes. The room was large, with French doors leading out to a patio on one end, a rolltop desk with a computer at the other, an unused fireplace with a faded wood mantel, and a chipped tile hearth, and not much else. One tiny, tired-looking oak bookcase overflowed with books, periodicals, and papers, along with a few office supplies. The rest of the room featured untidy piles of books and notes.

"I want this room to be a real office," he explained. "The plans you sent over are perfect. You can do one of those rolling staircases, right?"

"Most definitely. When I'm done, you'll have the prettiest office in all of Marlena."

"Pretty is fine, but I'm mainly interested in function. I'll be using this office to research and write a medical textbook, and I need a place to organize my source material."

"I can see that."

He ventured a look at her. She'd stepped behind

his desk to examine the wall, knocking on it. Then she pulled a small electronic gizmo from the pocket of her striped overalls and ran it along the wall, pausing to make a pencil mark.

"What's that?" he asked.

"A stud finder."

Look no farther, darlin', I'm right here. He couldn't help his thoughts. Hell, he'd almost said it out loud. She was so pretty—even though he suspected she wasn't trying. No makeup, no jewelry... He wished she would get out from behind his desk so he could see the rest of her.

"So...do you have a father or brother who does the actual building?" he asked.

Those soft blue eyes took on the look of a summer rain cloud. "My father's deceased. It's just me. I'm the Kilgore of Kilgore Carpentry."

"But..."

"Yes?"

He supposed he didn't need to point out to Ms. Susan Kilgore that she was a woman. And he would sound like a Neanderthal if he expressed doubts about her abilities simply because she was female. He'd been in these situations enough in the past to know he had an uncanny ability to stick his foot right in his mouth.

"Um, will you excuse me?"

"Of course."

Rand headed for the kitchen, where he found Clark pouring sauce from a small pan into a Tupperware dish filled with some unidentifiable lumps. It wasn't very pretty, but the smell made Rand's mouth water.

"Take a look at this," Clark said. He wore a tall white hat and apron, which only served to emphasize his huge muscles. "Chitterlings and portabello mushrooms sautéed in a white wine—"

"Chitterlings!" Rand said in alarm. "I'll pass, thanks."

"It's not for you, it's a project for class. We're each supposed to take a family recipe and make it French."

"Your mother never made chitterlings."

Clark grinned. "Oh, yes, she did. We just told you it was something else. You want a taste?"

"No, thanks." Rand got to the point. "Did you know you hired a woman to build my bookcases?"

"Oh. She's here, huh?" Clark looked distinctly guilty as he snapped the lid over his masterpiece.

"Yes, she's here! And I can't see how she can do the work. Carpentry involves a lot of heavy lifting, power tools…"

Clark set the pan in the sink and ran water into it. "Look, Rand. I had doubts, too, when she told me her…situation. But she knows her stuff. And she sounded, you know, kind of desperate. Apparently not many people have given her a chance to prove herself."

"But this is my office we're talking about. My bookshelves."

"Well, you can't fire her now. You signed the contract."

"You tricked me! I'll...I'll pay her off."

"Can you look her in those big blue eyes and tell her she's fired?"

Rand narrowed his gaze. "How do you know she has big blue eyes?"

"I've met her. She and her dad redid my mom's staircase a couple years ago."

"Well, you hired her, you can fire her."

Clark glanced at his watch. "Golly gosh, look at the time. I'll be late for class."

"Clark!"

Clark whipped off his chef's clothes in record time, grabbed his Tupperware, and scooted out the back door, ignoring Rand's objections.

"Well, hell," Rand muttered. Better get it over with.

He returned to his office to find Susan with her back to him, stretching a tape measure up to the ceiling. He'd always thought a woman in overalls was kind of cute. She squatted to run the tape measure to the floor, and the denim pulled tight across her bottom.

She had a really nice bottom.

Oh, Lord, he didn't want to fire her. Even if he offered to pay off the contract, her feelings would be hurt. Maybe...maybe he could at least give her a chance. He would keep a close eye on her work, of course. No harm in that, was there? If at any time it seemed she wasn't performing up to par, he could pull the plug then.

She seemed to have some trouble standing. She had

to grab onto the edge of the desk and pull herself up, conjuring up a familiar scene from Rand's memory. He'd seen a woman make exactly that movement before...

She turned, startled, when he cleared his throat, and her difficulty suddenly made sense.

"You're...you're..." Rand sputtered.

"I think the word you're looking for is pregnant."

SUSAN WINCED IN anticipation of the explosion. She was busted, she knew it. Rand Barclay was going to throw her out, contract or no contract, and she had no recourse unless she wanted to sue him.

Clark had warned her that Dr. Barclay was something of a curmudgeon, a man immersed in his work with little use for outside distractions. She hadn't expected him to be such a hunk, though, with that raven-black hair flopping over his forehead and those piercing blue eyes, even bluer than her own. Even Gary, her ex-boyfriend, who'd had a blond, beach-bum sort of charm about him, didn't hold a candle to this guy. With those wide shoulders and big biceps, she could picture him on the racquetball court or paddling a kayak through white water. But in a white coat behind a microscope?

She glanced over to the blank wall where she'd just made her pencil marks where the studs were. It was completely radical of her to think she could do this job when she was pregnant. But she really needed the work, and with just a little help lifting the heavier pieces, she could achieve fantastic results—if only Rand would give her a chance.

But her hopes plummeted as she studied his face, which looked like thunder. "Did Clark know when he hired you?"

"Yes. I was completely honest with him."

"I'll kill him."

She straightened her spine, prepared to do battle. "Don't blame Clark. He said no at first, but I talked him into it."

"Well, you won't talk me into it. I will not have a pregnant woman doing heavy manual labor in my house."

"But I can do this, I promise I can."

"Do you have any help?"

"No. Look, I've been working with wood since I was five, Dr. Barclay."

"I'm not questioning your skills. But you can't possibly build a massive project like this when you're... How far along are you, anyway?"

"About seven months," she fudged. Really she was closer to eight, but she didn't look that far along.

"How are you going to lift big pieces of lumber and climb ladders in your condition?"

"I've checked with my nurse-practitioner. I know my limitations. Besides, I've been working out at the gym every day. I'm strong as a broodmare. The harder I work, the better I feel. Just...just please give me a chance. I'm sure people have believed in you your whole life, but I haven't had that luxury."

"Doesn't your husband object to your doing this kind of work?"

Susan fingered the plain gold band on her left hand. It was her mother's. She'd started wearing it when she got tired of explaining to people that she didn't have a husband.

She could tell Rand the truth—that she wasn't married and never had been, that the father of her baby had abandoned her before he even knew she was pregnant, that she was all alone in the world and nothing stood between her and the street except this job.

But she didn't want his pity. She wanted him to have faith in her. "My husband is not a problem."

He looked down at his shoes. Was it possible she was making headway? She decided to press her advantage, if she did indeed have one.

"Although the shelves and cabinetry look massive on paper, this particular project doesn't require much heavy work, and Clark promised to help. The lumberyard will do all the big cuts for me, so I won't have to lift whole pieces of lumber or anything like that."

"Do you have insurance?" he asked.

"Yes, of course. I can show you the policy—"

"No, that's not necessary." He paused, staring out the window. He seemed to be deliberating.

She held her breath. *Please, please, please.*

He came closer, until he was only a step away from her, and eyed her up and down, making her feel like he was the stallion to that broodmare she'd mentioned earlier. What did he see? And did he like it? And why was she even wondering something so stupid?

"I guess since I signed a contract, I have no choice."

She resisted the urge to throw her arms around him in gratitude and instead grasped both his hands. "You won't be sorry, I promise. I'll build you the best damn bookshelf you ever saw!"

"Um, yes, right." He extracted his hands from her enthusiastic grip. "But I don't want to see you endangering yourself or your baby. I mean that. Contract or no contract, I will throw you out in a New York minute if you so much as—"

"I won't."

"You'll be able to finish the job before your, er, family addition arrives, right?"

Susan felt a lump rising in her throat. *Family addition.* That was ironic, seeing as she had no family. She forced a smile. "This job should take two weeks—well, three, tops." And she was a good four weeks from her due date. That was cutting it a bit close, but she was pretty sure she could make it.

Chapter Two

"I just need to get my stepladder off the truck so I can finish the measurements," Susan said.

Rand felt like he'd just been through a tornado. Had he really agreed to let a pregnant woman build his bookcases? But she was damn persuasive. He could see now why Clark had caved in to her—and why he'd acted so guilty and made such a quick escape.

"I'll carry the ladder," he said firmly. "Then I'll climb it for you."

"That's not really necessary," she said with equal firmness. "The ladder isn't heavy, and I've been climbing it since before I could walk."

"But your equilibrium has changed."

"I've adjusted."

Rand didn't argue. He'd learned over the years that arguing with a woman was fruitless. He simply walked outside with her and grabbed the ladder.

"I can get that," she insisted, standing with her arms folded stubbornly. She stood right in his way, so that he couldn't slide the ladder out of its rack without physically picking her up and moving her. With a shrug he stepped back and let her slide the ladder off the truck. She didn't seem to be straining, so he let her carry it, though he was bewildered by her behavior.

His mother had been single through most of his childhood—her second husband hadn't stuck around much longer than Rand's own father. So Rand had helped raise his three half sisters and spent most of his formative years as the only male in the family.

But females were still an alien species to him. He'd tried to understand them, really he had. But usually when he engaged them in conversation, they either stared blankly at him or talked a mile a minute about something that made no sense to him.

Even his sisters fell into that category. There just didn't seem to be a connection between the functioning of the female brain and his own.

He hovered as Susan set up the ladder. "You're sure you don't want me to—"

"I can do it," she said with a confident smile. "I'm only going up two steps. It's not like I'm scaling the Sears Tower." And for no good reason, she smiled. That smile totally blew him away. It lit up her whole face, making him wonder what her hair would look like down, free from the no-nonsense ponytail.

Whoa. Rand put the skids on that line of thought. Susan Kilgore was attractive—he'd have to be dead not to notice. But she obviously belonged to another man, so there was no chance of any chemistry between them. Not that he'd want that. He had a book to write, and he wanted no distractions.

Those eyes could distract the Devil himself....

"I'm nearby if you need anything." He moved closer to his desk, but his work held no interest when another, more alluring view tempted him.

She climbed the ladder sideways so her full stomach didn't get in the way, and she seemed completely comfortable—no wobbling.

He wished she'd let him help. The idea of building something with this woman, working side by side with her, was oddly appealing.

That was bizarre, he thought as he flipped through a stack of Web pages he'd printed out and stacked them by subject matter. He'd spent a great deal of time with females and had certainly done his share of dating. He appreciated the female form—in all its variations, apparently, given his physical reaction to Susan. But he was always happiest if he could take a woman to a movie or concert where they didn't have to talk. Even better if they could just cut to the chase and go to bed. Lately he hadn't even bothered. His liaisons never lasted, and the awkward gropings in the dark that had once satisfied his libido now left him unfulfilled.

He realized he was a dinosaur. Men these days talked to their women. They engaged in deep, meaningful conversations about their relationship, and if they couldn't, they went to therapy. Even Clark, who'd been the most macho member of the Georgia Tech football team a few years back, often spent hours at a time talking with Deirdre, his girlfriend. When Rand asked Clark what they talked about, Clark just shrugged and said, "Everything under the sun." And he got a stupid smile on his face.

"Rand?"

He was at her side in an instant. "Is something wrong?"

"I just thought, since you want to help, you could hold the tape measure for me."

"Oh. Sure." Their fingers brushed as she handed him her industrial-sized metal tape measure. He kept a wary eye on her while she stretched the tape this way and that and recorded the measurements on a pocket computer.

What was that scent she wore? Vanilla? Peaches? He'd never been very good at telling one girly smell apart from another.

She moved with incredible grace for a pregnant woman. The fact that she was moving at all amazed him. When his sisters had been in their last trimester, they'd hardly been able to make it from the couch to the kitchen.

"I'm not keeping you from something, am I?" Susan asked. "Clark said you were working on some important medical textbook."

He didn't really want to talk about his work. The minute he mentioned to a woman what he really did for a living, her eyes glazed over.

"What kind of doctor are you, anyway?" she continued, oblivious to his reticence.

"I'm a dermatologist," he admitted. Dermatology

had to be one of the least glamorous medical disciplines, right up there with urology.

"But I don't see patients anymore," he said. "I work strictly in the lab doing research."

"On what?" she wanted to know.

"Not a cure for cancer or anything so glamorous. I'm studying allergic skin rashes." Which was where most people's curiosity came to an abrupt halt—unless they happened to be the victim of a troublesome rash, in which case he got more details about it than he ever cared to know.

Susan didn't vary from the norm. "Someone's got to study rashes, I suppose." She returned her attention to her work.

Another scintillating conversation. Why did he have such a hard time with this? Not that it really mattered. He might be attracted to Susan—and let's face it, he was, regardless of her state of pregnancy—but she was completely out of reach.

SUSAN ARRIVED AT Rand's house early the next morning, eager to get to work. As she climbed out of her truck, her stomach seemed suddenly huge to her, straining against her striped overalls. Had she grown overnight? She found herself wishing she could wear one of those cute little Empire-waist maternity dresses she'd seen in the window at a shop downtown. Wearing those breezy floral fabrics, lined with delicate lace, even a woman the size of a small hippopotamus could feel feminine.

In her overalls, Susan just felt fat and ungainly. It hadn't really bothered her before now.

Rand opened the front door before she could even knock. He wore a pristine white lab coat, open at the front to reveal a blue shirt and silk tie, making Susan more positive than ever that scientists weren't as nerdy as their stereotypes suggested. And he carried a fragrant cup of coffee, making her despise him.

She wanted coffee, damn it.

"Good morning," she said. "Is Clark around?"

"Why do you need him?" Rand asked bluntly.

"He promised to help me carry in this lumber and my tools." She hated having to ask.

"I'll do it."

"But you'll get your nice white coat all dirty."

"I wear the nice white coat so I don't get my clothes dirty. That's what lab coats are for." He sat his coffee down on the porch railing and flexed his arms above his head.

Holy cow, did he have any idea what he was doing to her already messed-up hormones? The soft blue button-down shirt he wore stretched and strained against his chest, and he seemed oblivious to the stiff northern breeze that blew today, bringing a touch of winter to the Carolinas.

His attitude was hardly cheerful, but Susan wasn't going to complain. He hadn't fired her yet.

Rand wouldn't hear of her carrying anything, even the smaller pieces of wood. Since he was writing the checks, she let him have the last word, but she wasn't happy about it. She'd promised herself she would never, ever lean on a man again.

Phrases from Gary's "Dear Jane" letter drifted into her consciousness: *clinging vine...dependent...draining all my energy...parasite.*

She would be the first to admit she'd been a little crazy when she'd lived with Gary. He'd met her at the hospital just minutes after she'd witnessed her father's life slip away. She'd been distraught, unsure what to do next, and he'd simply taken her under his wing and made all her decisions for her.

What a relief it had been, after her father's long illness and the money problems and business problems, to simply let go. Gary had *wanted* her to depend on him. Falling in love with him had been effortless—how could she not fall in love with a handsome white knight who was right there all the time to slay even her smallest dragons?

Unfortunately, she'd continued to lean on him long after the trauma of losing her father. He'd just made it so damn easy—he'd encouraged it. She thought that was what he wanted, and she wanted more than anything to make him happy after all he'd done for her.

Her devotion had backfired in a big way. She'd had no idea she was driving him crazy. Her first clue was when she'd come home from her doctor's appointment and found the note.

She'd not seen him again. He'd disappeared like a soap bubble in the wind, completely ignorant of the fact that he would shortly be a father.

"I don't want to make you late for work," Susan

said to Rand as she trotted after him on his third trip from the truck to the house. "I can take it from here."

"I think I'll stay home today. Now might be a good time to get some writing done."

"While I'm working? I'll be kicking up sawdust and making a lot of awful noise."

"I've got to at least get the books out of your way so you have enough room to work," Rand persisted.

Since this was true, she almost let it slide. Then something occurred to her. "You don't trust me."

"Of course I trust you," he said easily as he reclaimed his coffee cup on their final trip.

"You don't. You're going to keep an eye on me and make sure I don't mess up."

"Not true. I need a day off."

"Then take the day off! Go to the zoo or something."

He didn't go away. He lurked, he hovered, he tried to help her lift pieces of wood that a butterfly could have carried off.

"Did it ever occur to you," she asked, "that I might enjoy the feeling of accomplishment I get from doing a job on my own?"

"You won't like the feeling of a strained back," he said. "You pull something out of whack now, you might not be able to pick up your own baby."

All right, so he had a point. Though she was always careful—her father had suffered with numerous back problems and she didn't want to end up like that— she should be taking extra precautions at this time.

She let him pick up the blasted board and hold it in place.

After a while, it became easier to just let him do what he wanted. She would never get this job done if she argued with him every step of the way.

Besides, she sort of liked looking at him, especially later in the day when his sleeves were rolled up and his hair mussed, and she could detect the slight odor of hard work on a clean man.

RAND SPENT THE ENTIRE morning trying to find an excuse to fire Susan. He watched her every move, searching for some sign of incompetence—a corner that didn't meet cleanly, a board that had been mis-measured, or holes that weren't drilled in the exact right places. But he could find no fault in the woman's work. She knew what she was doing.

He also looked for signs that this work was too hard for a pregnant woman. But Susan had endless stamina and energy to spare—and she seemed to enjoy her work. She often smiled while she worked, or whistled, or hummed. He liked that she didn't fill the silence between them with useless prattle.

She didn't talk endlessly about her pregnancy the way his sisters had. She didn't probe into his personal life, but she did show an interest in his work.

Whether her fascination was genuine or merely polite, it flattered him. Most people groaned and changed the subject.

By the second day, Rand decided to ask a personal question of his own. She'd been evasive when he'd brought up the subject before, and he hadn't pressed for more information. Now was a better time.

"What does your husband do?"

Susan nearly dropped her screwdriver. He'd evidently startled her. "He's an engineer," she answered, recovering her poise quickly, "but he left his job recently..." She shrugged, then returned her attention to the drawer she was building.

An engineer. Didn't they make buckets of money? It sounded like maybe he'd been laid off and was unemployed. Surely he hadn't voluntarily left a decent job when his wife was expecting a baby.

Clearly Susan didn't want to talk about her husband, so Rand let it be. He hoped that, whatever her domestic problems were, they weren't too serious. A new baby brought a lot of stress into a home even under the best conditions—and didn't he know it. Still, it sounded as if Susan was underappreciated at home, at the very least. Hell, if she was *his* wife...

What a completely weird thought. If Susan's husband had any idea Rand found her so alluring, he'd come over here and flatten Rand.

That night after she left, the house was incredibly quiet. No crying babies, no feminine chatter, no power tools, not even anyone puttering in the kitchen. Clark had just left for an early date with Dierdre.

A perfect time to start organizing those books, Rand thought. He and Susan had merely moved stacks from one side of the room to the other, then covered them with plastic.

Rand returned to the office and peeled back the

plastic. He would put the medical texts in one area, organized by subject. Then the journals. He ought to get a file box for those untidy clippings and photocopies. And all those computer printouts—he ought to get a special box for those, too. Then there were the photographs....

He'd better make a trip to the office supply store. No time like the present. And Clark thought he procrastinated. Hah!

WHEN SUSAN ARRIVED the next morning, she was surprised to find a host of different colored file boxes, accordion files, folders, dividers. Rand sat at his rolltop desk, unwrapping packages of colored pens, selfsticking notepads of various sizes, reams of computer paper.

"Looks like you wiped out the office supply store."

He looked up. "Oh, hi. I just thought the organizing would go better if I had the proper tools."

"Uh-huh. I'm sure you're right."

"Now don't you start on me. Clark says I'm procrastinating again. I tried to explain to him that it was the same thing as trying to cook a gourmet dinner for twelve without all the ingredients and the right cookware. Or like you building a bookshelf without the right woods and tools. You can't just jump into these things half-cocked."

Susan picked up a small piece of wood and started hand sanding a sharp corner. "Of course not," she said soothingly. "Out of curiosity, how long have you been researching?"

"Oh, I don't know. A couple of years."

"So, how does that work? Does someone pay you to do the research?"

"I have a grant from the National Institutes of Health and Harvard Medical School."

"Do you have a deadline or something?"

"Actually, I was supposed to have a draft to committee by the end of this month, but I've gotten a deadline extension." He flipped on his computer. "I wonder if I need a new word processing program."

What he needed, Susan thought, was a kick in the butt to make him start working. But it was none of her business. "I'm getting ready to make sawdust. You probably want to turn off the computer and cover it."

"Oh, right. I was going to start working on my introduction, but I guess that can wait."

"You could take one of those new legal pads and sit outside to write," she suggested.

"Good idea." Rand puttered around his desk, selecting a pad and the right pen. But somehow he never got out of the office. He kept finding little things to do, small ways to help Susan. Before she knew it, Clark was calling them to lunch.

Susan felt ridiculous, sitting in the formal dining room in her dusty overalls, eating with real china and silver. But she couldn't argue with the food. Clark managed to make a simple chicken salad into a work of gastronomic art. Even the pile of potato chips on her plate were an exotic, multicolored affair. Left to her own devices, she probably would have made do with a cheese sandwich.

"Do you eat like this every day?" she couldn't help asking Rand. "If Clark was cooking for me, I'd be big as a—never mind."

Her face heated, especially when she noticed Rand looking determinedly down at his plate, fighting a smile.

"Oh, go ahead and say what you're thinking," she groused. "I'm already as big as a house."

"Just a small house," Rand said.

Clark, who was just sitting down to join them, stared at Rand. "Did you just make a joke?" Then he looked at Susan. "I think he made a joke, don't you? Let's see, the last time that happened was nineteen—"

"Oh, knock it off," Rand said. "Susan's going to think I'm an ogre."

"He's not an ogre," Clark hastened to say. "He's just been acting like one ever since Alicia and Dougy moved out."

Susan's ears pricked up. She had gathered Rand wasn't married. Had his marriage recently broken up?

"My sister and her son," Rand clarified. "Don't listen to Clark. I've been all sweetness and light. After eight years, all of my sisters are financially independent of me and I finally have the place to myself. Alicia just moved in with her fiancé, and I couldn't be happier."

Personally, Susan thought living in a house this

size all by yourself, or even with Clark, would be a waste. This was a house meant for families. She wondered why Rand had chosen to be alone. He didn't seem antisocial. Had he been badly hurt by a woman?

RAND *WANTED* TO WORK on his book, he really did. But he found it difficult to concentrate with Susan in the same room. He found himself staring at her, fascinated. Although at first he'd thought her hands unattractive, after he'd spent hours watching them gripping a power tool or running lightly over a piece of wood to check the smoothness of its grain, he completely changed his mind. He couldn't recall ever being attracted to strength and manual dexterity in a woman, but he couldn't deny he enjoyed those things about Susan Kilgore—in a very visceral way.

Of course, he would never let on that he was even mildly attracted to her. She obviously had no use for him.

The rest of the week passed without incident. Susan made steady progress on the bookshelves, and Rand started to feel almost comfortable around her. She didn't demand from him the incomprehensible things other women wanted. He wasn't required to show interest in subjects that bored him. She did not expect him to solve her problems. He didn't have to spend money on her, other than what was contracted. She certainly had no designs on his body, thank God.

She was...nonthreatening. Food for his fantasies, and nothing more.

But the fantasies—those were wild. Sometimes he

couldn't help remembering her scent, or thinking about what her hair would feel like tickling his chest, or other, more earthy things. This wasn't the sort of pointless activity he normally engaged in—especially regarding a woman who was claimed by another man in so obvious a way. But he seemed helpless to stop the alluring thoughts.

On Monday morning, however, she arrived at his house in an inexplicably hellacious mood. She cursed at the wood, at her tools, at herself for being clumsy. She ordered him out of the room twice, but he managed to wander back in.

He should have gone into the lab, since he was getting nothing accomplished at home. But he'd promised Alicia he would baby-sit Dougy this morning while she went on a job interview, and she was due to arrive any time.

"Is there anything I can do?" he asked Susan mildly.

"Just stay out of my way." Then she dropped her hammer and doubled over in pain.

Chapter Three

No, it couldn't be, Susan thought as she knelt clutching her abdomen.

"Susan!"

Rand was at her side in an instant. "Don't stop breathing. That's it, relax.... Is this what I think it is?"

"It can't be," Susan said when she could talk. The pain subsided after a few seconds, almost as if it had never been there. "It's three weeks early!"

"Okay, don't panic," Rand said soothingly. "Does it—three weeks? I thought you said you were—"

"I, um, stretched the truth a little. I figured the less pregnant you thought I was, the better my chances of keeping this job."

"Oh, *hell.*" He looked like he wanted to wring her neck, and the only thing preventing him was her physical distress. "So did that *feel* like a labor pain?"

"How would I know? I've never had one before."

"Does it feel like you imagine labor pains might feel?" he persisted, though he did help her to her feet and lead her over to one of the club chairs. He whipped the plastic off and made her sit down. Then he claimed the other chair and peered at her till she felt compelled to answer.

"It felt like a big hand grabbed me around my middle and squeezed as hard as it could." And it had scared the bejeezus out of her.

"That sounds like a labor pain, all right."

"How would you know?" She wasn't sure why she was being so cross with him. It seemed easier to bear her fear by masking it with anger.

"First, I'm a doctor," he said, as if explaining something to an idiot. "Delivering babies isn't my specialty, but I had to do an obstetrics rotation just like every other doctor. And second, my three sisters have five children among them, and I was there when every single one of them went into labor."

"How did you manage that?"

"Because my sisters—they spend a lot of time here. How many babies have *you* watched being born?"

"Okay, okay."

"Feeling better now?" The lines of his face had relaxed slightly.

"Yes. I feel perfectly fine. I think it must have been a fluke. Something I ate."

"Possibly," he said, sounding doubtful. "Have you felt anything else strange this morning? Any sensations out of the ordinary?"

She had. Her lower back had been aching, but she'd figured that was perfectly normal, given the punishment she'd put her body through the past few days. She'd also felt kind of a funny pressure, down there, but she didn't recall any mention of that as a precursor to labor in any of her maternity books, so she hadn't thought much of it. At any rate, she wasn't going to discuss that with Rand. It was much too personal, doctor or not.

"I've felt fine," she fibbed. "I'll just get back to work." She stood, despite Rand's troubled frown, and retrieved the hammer she'd dropped. She resumed work and after a couple of minutes managed to convince herself everything was fine, though Rand had not moved from his chair and he continued to study her like she was one of his lab experiments.

Then another pain gripped her, stronger than the first. She nearly fell over from the force of it. But Rand was suddenly there, his hands on her shoulders steadying her.

"Easy, there. Another one?"

"Uh-huh."

"Okay, just go with it. Don't fight it. Breathe, relax…"

Her breathing was more like gasping, and she whimpered like a kicked dog, much to her embarrassment. But Rand just kept murmuring gentle encouragements to her. She focused on the soothing sound of his voice, the feel of his big hands on her shoulders, and after a few moments she realized the pain had receded.

"All right now?" he asked, practically dragging her back to the chair she'd just vacated.

She nodded.

"Then let's get you to the hospital. Which one were you planning to use?"

"None of them," she admitted. "I was planning to have a home birth, with a midwife. And that's still what I want."

RAND JUST STARED AT Susan. It took a few moments for what she'd said to sink in. Home birth? He knew that was an increasingly popular choice, but he'd never personally known anyone who did it.

"It's a perfectly legitimate alternative to hospital births," she said, crossing her arms defensively over her stomach. "My midwife is a nurse-practitioner. I've been healthy as a horse throughout the whole pregnancy, so I'm a perfect candidate."

"You're three weeks early."

His one statement diminished everything she'd said, and she knew it. He could tell by the way she didn't meet his gaze.

He grabbed the phone and handed it to her. "Why don't you call your midwife and see what she has to say?" He knew he was taking a chance. But if the woman really was a trained nurse-practitioner, she knew as well as he did the increased risks a premature birth entailed, especially for the baby. He handed Susan the phone.

Home birth? Not in his home she wasn't.

She made the call, and he busied himself at his desk sharpening his new pencils with the new noiseless pencil sharpener he'd just bought. After a couple of minutes she put down the phone, looking defeated.

"Arnette agrees with you. She said she'll meet me at Savannah City. She participates in a midwife program there."

Relief washed through Rand. As an M.D., he knew he was somewhat prejudiced, but birth outside of a sterile hospital delivery room sounded almost barbaric to him in this day and age.

"Savannah City has an excellent obstetrics unit," he said as he helped her out of her chair. "You can do all-natural childbirth, if you want. But they also have an excellent neonatal unit standing by."

Susan's eyes filled with tears. "Do you really think something will be wrong with her? What if they have to put her in one of those glass cases with all the tubes and needles—"

"I'm sure she'll be fine," he said, trying to convince himself as well as her. He didn't blame Susan for being frightened half out of her wits. He wasn't exactly calm himself.

Hell, he was a doctor. He wasn't supposed to be upset by a medical emergency. When any of his sisters had gone into labor, he was always the calm voice of reason. But none of them had been early.

"Where are we going?" she asked when he steered her toward the kitchen.

"The garage? My car? Or were you planning to hitchhike to Savannah?"

"You're going to drive me?"

"How else did you imagine you would get there?"

She blinked a couple of times. "Drive myself?" Another pain hit her then. She didn't howl the way his sisters had. She whimpered. And it just about tore his heart out.

The back of his neck prickled with fear.

After the pain had passed, Rand took Susan through the kitchen where Clark was basting a small roast chicken.

"I'm taking Susan to the hospital," Rand announced.

Clark grinned. "Why don't you just change your specialty to obstetrics?"

"Very funny. I don't think Susan appreciates jokes right now." He headed for the back door.

"Touchy, touchy." Clark shoved the roasting pan back into the oven and pulled off his apron. "It's not like you haven't done this drill a time or two. Hold on, don't leave without me."

"You're coming, too?" Susan asked.

"Rand'll need someone to drive so he can focus on vital signs and timing contractions and all that."

"All right, all right, hurry up," Rand said. He hit the garage door opener just as a familiar Jeep pulled into the driveway. Oh, *hell*. It was Alicia and Dougy.

Gesturing wildly as if her car were a 747, he guided his sister into a parking space so she wouldn't block his exit from the garage. "Clark, get Susan settled into the back seat of the Bronco. Alicia!" he called as his sister exited her car. "No time to explain. Put Dougy's car seat in the back of the Bronco. He can go to Savannah with us."

Alicia, dressed in jeans and a sweatshirt, did not look ready for a job interview. "Savannah?"

"To the hospital," he explained. "Hurry up! Can't you see this is an emergency?"

Alicia looked at Susan. "You're having a baby?"

"It appears so."

"Oh, what great fun!" Alicia said excitedly. "Can we go? My job interview got rescheduled."

"Susan's labor is not a spectator event!" Rand objected. It felt like everyone was moving in slow motion. Was he the only one feeling the raw edges of panic?

"I'm great in a crisis," Alicia said, appealing straight to Susan. "I went through this less than two years ago, so I know everything. I'm Rand's sister, Alicia, by the way. Do you want me to come?"

Susan managed a smile. "Sure, the more the merrier."

Rand threw up his hands in defeat. They all piled into the Bronco, Clark driving, Alicia in the passenger seat, Dougy, Rand, and Susan in back.

"No one has to give me directions," Clark said, taking off.

Savannah was forty-five minutes away. Susan's contractions came with reassuring regularity, about five minutes apart. That meant she was definitely in labor, Rand told her. In his most doctorlike voice, he assured her there was plenty of time, but he felt more like a nervous, first-time father than a seasoned medical professional.

He hadn't felt this nervous even when he was a clueless kid, driving his mother to the hospital—with no driver's license—so she could have Alicia. What was it about Susan that made him so afraid for her?

Halfway to Savannah, something occurred to Rand. "My God, Susan, we haven't even called your husband! Someone give me a cell phone. I'll dial it for you."

"I've got one," Alicia said brightly, digging through her purse. "It's in here somewhere."

"That's all right," Susan said. "I, um, won't be able to get in touch with him now, anyway."

"You mean he can't be reached?" Rand asked, incensed. "Isn't he the least bit worried about you? Doesn't he have a beeper or something?"

Susan shook her head. "I'll call him...later."

Something was funny about her reaction. She did not seem overjoyed at the prospect of telling her husband he was about to be a daddy. And was she crying?

"Oh, all right, you might as well know," she said, sniffing back tears. "I don't have a husband to call."

A stunned silence followed Susan's announcement. Rand was more than surprised. All this time he'd thought Susan was so *safe,* so...so untouchable. He'd actually started feeling comfortable around her. A pregnant, married woman was no threat at all. But a pregnant, *single* woman...

"You lied to me about that, too?"

SUSAN HAD BEEN HOPING she wouldn't have to reveal to Rand that she was an unwed mother—it was so embarrassing. She'd figured she'd be done with the bookshelves and far away from Rand before he could discover the truth.

But she couldn't continue with the farce of the fictional husband.

She looked at him. He didn't meet her gaze, and the expression on his face was impenetrable. Had she shocked him? Disgusted him? He definitely did not seem pleased with her news.

"Everything I told you about Gary was true," she said. "Except he was never my husband. And he's gone."

"I know just what you're going through," Alicia piped in, breaking the awkward tension. "Dougy's birth father wasn't around either. But with all my own family to take up the slack, I hardly noticed anybody missing. I had six labor coaches, counting Clark."

Susan relaxed a little. Rand's sister, a short-haired pixie with huge, dark eyes, was an absolute delight, and she, at least, would stop the others from tossing her out on the side of the road. "It sounds like your family is very supportive."

"And I'm sure yours will be, too. Here, why don't you call everybody you know?" Alicia handed her the phone.

Susan didn't take it. "I don't really have anybody to call." It was painful to admit it, but she had no one. She was an only child, and both parents were deceased. She had some distant relatives in Illinois, but that was it. As for friends, she had let them fall by the wayside when she'd gotten so wrapped up in her relationship with Gary. And after he'd left, she'd just folded in on herself. The only person she'd confided in lately was Arnette, her midwife, who was the closest thing she had to a friend, and Mrs. Regis.

Alicia, craning around to look at her, wore an expression of sympathy. "We'll be your family, then, won't we, guys? Babies are such exciting events. And the Barclay family knows how to do it up right. I'll call Betty and Bonnie, too. They'll want to come."

"Alicia!" Rand scolded. "Why don't you call Mom while you're at it?"

"Oh, now, *that* would be a treat." Alicia started pushing buttons on the phone.

Rand pulled the phone out of her hands. "You're not calling anyone. Susan doesn't even know us! I'm sure she doesn't want a bunch of strangers around while she's having a baby."

Susan wanted to correct him. For some odd reason, she *did* want a lot of people around. For all these months, she hadn't exactly viewed her pregnancy with joy. It had been more of a problem to overcome, a strategic challenge. Still, sometimes, when the baby kicked inside, Susan would feel a wave of affection for the life she was bringing into the world.

She knew she would find the reserves to be a good mother. But there'd been no giddy anticipation, no real excitement, just a lot of apprehension about how she would take care of this child when her own life was such a mess.

The idea of a bunch of excited people hanging around to talk her through the pain, to rejoice with her over the birth, to *ooh* and *aah* over the newborn, had an inordinate amount of appeal.

And the idea that Rand would be one of those people, maybe holding her hand, whispering encouragement in her ear, giving her ice chips, mopping her sweaty brow, was the most appealing aspect of all.

Now, what was wrong with this picture? Rand was her client. She'd lied to him about several things, and now he'd been shanghaied into shuttling her to the hospital. That didn't exactly qualify him as her labor coach. But the fantasy had lodged itself in her mind and wouldn't be evicted.

Another contraction hit her, much stronger than the others had been. She let out a yelp, then censored herself.

"Oh, for heaven's sake, let it out," Alicia said. "Scream like a banshee. Everybody expects it, and you'll get more sympathy."

Susan laughed through tears of pain. "I don't want to scream. It's so undignified."

"Undignified, unshmignified," Alicia returned. "All the books tell you it hurts—they just don't tell you how much."

"You got that right."

"It hurts more than when I broke my arm in third grade."

"It hurts a lot more than when I had a root canal," Susan added.

"I've heard passing a kidney stone hurts worse," Clark added.

"Only a man would say that," Alicia said. "Hurts worse than having your legs waxed."

"Hurts worse than cutting your finger almost all the way off with a band saw," Susan said.

"Have you done that?"

"See the scar? I was five." She extended her hand for Alicia's inspection. Silly as their game was, it did take her mind off the pain, and her fear. *God, please let the baby be all right.*

"Who are you, anyway?" Alicia suddenly asked, softening the abrupt question with a laugh. "Rand's obviously been hiding a secret or two from us."

"Alicia!" Rand exploded. "She's not my secret. She's my carpenter. She's building a shelving unit in the office."

"Oh." Alicia gave her brother an appraising look, as if she didn't quite believe *that* story. She looked at Susan. "You're redoing his office?"

Susan didn't answer because another contraction hit. Dougy, who'd been remarkably quiet and well-behaved, studied her curiously from his car seat as she panted her way through the pain.

Rand answered Alicia's question. "Don't you think it's about time I turned that room back into an office? My nieces and nephews have laid waste to it for seven years. Anyway, I've got a real need for it now."

"Ah, yes, the infamous skin-rash term paper."

"Jeez, I get no respect. It's a textbook."

The argument ended there, because they'd arrived at the hospital.

THE MOMENT SUSAN WAS spirited away to her labor room, a woman thrust a clipboard at Rand. "You'll need to fill out these forms, sir."

"Oh, I'm not the husband…father…whatever."

"Then where is he?"

"He won't be here," Rand said, unable to communicate Susan's unwed state without feeling like a gossip.

"Well, her next of kin will need to fill out these papers."

With a sign of resignation, Rand took the clipboard. "I'll take care of it."

A few minutes later, after Susan was firmly ensconced in her cozy labor/delivery room, Rand broached her about the papers. "I can fill them out, if you'll tell me what to write," he offered.

"I guess we have to," she said uneasily.

The first part went smoothly enough. Name, address, phone. For "person to notify in case of emergency," she thought a long while, then said, "Harriet Regis" and rattled off a phone number.

"Anyone else?" Rand asked.

"No." She had another contraction, and her water broke. Arnette, the midwife, arrived and talked her through it. Meanwhile, Rand stepped off into a corner and wrote in his own name and phone as a second emergency contact. Just in case.

Rand waited until Alicia and Clark left to find some coffee and Arnette went outside to take a phone call before asking Susan about insurance—the next set of papers to be filled out.

She sighed gustily. "That's why I wanted to do this at home. I don't have any."

"Insurance? You don't have any at all? You told me you did!"

"I have liability insurance," she answered softly. "And I have health insurance, too, but it doesn't cover the pregnancy. I signed up for it too late."

Rand didn't know quite what to say to that. Having a baby was an expensive proposition, medically speaking. Costs would skyrocket if there were any problems with her or the baby...no, he didn't want to think about that. He was less nervous now that Susan was safely hospitalized, but his mouth still felt like he'd just eaten five Saltines at once, and his heart still beat at twice its normal rhythm.

"I know what you're thinking," she said, "that it's completely irresponsible for anybody to get pregnant without insurance."

"Sometimes life doesn't go according to our plans," he said diplomatically, though he was aghast at Susan's mounting misfortunes.

"Well, I'm not irresponsible. My...Gary, the baby's father, left quite unexpectedly. He quit the company he was working for and let them cancel both of our insurance policies without telling me."

"When you were pregnant?" Rand sputtered. How could anyone be that coldhearted?

"He didn't know I was pregnant. I was going to tell him, and then he was gone, and I was such a mess it was a couple of months before I even thought about insurance. By then it was too late."

"It seems to me he ought to be held accountable for your medical expenses," Rand said with a lot more control than he felt inside. A decent man doesn't put a woman in danger like that. But Gary obviously wasn't decent if he could care so little for Susan's welfare. Kind of like Rand's own father, now that he thought about it.

"I agree," Susan said. "Only one problem. I can't find him."

"You've tried?"

"Yes. For months. He left me a note asking me not to contact him, and he took great pains to make sure I couldn't find him. Even his former co-workers play dumb."

"What about his family?"

She shrugged. "I don't know where they are, either. We'd only been living together for about six months. I'd never met his family. He was sort of vague about them, hinting around that they weren't on the best of terms."

"His family probably disowned him." Rand wondered if Gary made a habit of collecting women, dumping them after a few months, and disappearing. He refrained from saying anything else negative, but only to spare distressing Susan further.

"You don't really want to find him, do you?" Rand asked.

"Yes. Yes, I really do." Her eyes shined—with excitement or tears, he wasn't sure. "Every child should have a chance to know his or her father."

At her animated answer, Rand's heart sank a little.

He knew enough from his psych rotation to understand why he felt the inappropriate disappointment. He had become, at least temporarily, the most important person in Susan's life. He did not enjoy the idea of this Gary reappearing in her life and suddenly taking over.

He could find Gary for her. He had resources she didn't have—money, contacts. But he wasn't going to make the effort. She was so much better off without the bum—didn't she realize that?

Damn! Why did he suddenly feel so protective of her? She was an adult, not a child, not one of his sisters to be guided through a rough patch in her life.

They went back to the forms, and she recounted her medical history, which was surprisingly sparse. Other than the accident with the saw, she'd never seen the inside of a hospital, and apparently had rarely seen a doctor. "I told you I was healthy as a horse," she said.

Then another contraction hit.

"Ow, ow, ow, *ow!*" She sobbed out a couple of curse words. Rand broke out in a sweat. This was the sort of outburst he was used to from seeing his sisters in labor, but it seemed more alarming coming from Susan, maybe because she'd been so stoic up to this point.

He was the only one in the room with her. He grabbed her hand. "Squeeze hard and count backward from twenty-five."

"What?"

"Do it."

She scrunched her eyes shut and squeezed his hand. "Twenty-five, twenty-four..." Suddenly she relaxed, loosening her grip.

"Bad one, huh?" He smoothed a loose strand of hair from her pale face, realizing too late how much like a caress his gesture was.

"Mmm." She nodded.

Arnette, a plump Polynesian woman with a reassuring smile, came back into the room. "How're you doing, sweetheart?"

Susan was still trying to catch her breath. "Feels like it's not a baby inside me, it's a buzz saw with a dull blade."

"We can get you some medicine, you know," Arnette said.

"No, I want to do it natural."

"Then I'm just going to check your dilation."

That was Rand's cue to leave. He grabbed the clipboard with the completed forms, then wandered downstairs, thinking he might locate some coffee. Instead he found himself in the business office, talking with the same clerk. He handed her the clipboard. She smiled her thanks, but the smile died on her lips as she glanced at the form.

"No insurance?"

"Um, no."

"She should be at the county hospital, not here," the woman said frostily. "We don't accept indigents."

"She's not—" Hell, he didn't feel like arguing. To

his utter amazement, he whipped out his credit card. "Put Ms. Kilgore's charges on here."

In for a penny, in for a pound.

THE NEXT FEW HOURS went by in a haze of antici-pation, pain and cold fear for Susan. Arnette was there, reassuring Susan in her lilting accent that ev-erything was progressing nicely. Clark and Alicia took turns telling her jokes. But nothing comforted her—nothing except Rand's presence.

She wasn't sure why she felt safer with him there. Maybe because he was a doctor, although it wasn't like she was suffering from prickly heat. She just knew that when she felt most afraid, sure something was wrong, positive the labor would go on for eter-nity, she would catch him from the corner of her eye and instantly feel calmer.

He even did all those things she'd fantasized about. He held her hand. He blotted the perspiration from her forehead. He fed her ice chips. During those in-creasingly long and frequent contractions, she felt his attention on her in a visceral way, almost like he was willing her pain away.

In her less sane moments, she fantasized he was her husband, the father of her child, and that when the baby was born they would be a family. She knew it was a juvenile rescue fantasy, but she allowed her-self to savor it. Anything to get through her labor, which really sucked, in her opinion.

At one minute to midnight, Penelope Kilgore made her appearance. Susan hadn't thought much about

names, but when Rand declared the newborn was
bright and shiny as a new penny, the name sort of
stuck. Penelope—Penny for short.

She was tiny—barely over five pounds—but she
was perfect in every way, or so Susan thought when
they put the baby into her arms. She was a miracle.
How could Gary not fall in love with this precious
scrap of life they had created, even if it was acciden-
tal?

Then a dose of reality hit her. This was real. She
was a mother, now, and she had this child to feed,
nurture and protect.

She looked up at Rand and forcefully dislodged the
fantasy that had gotten her through labor. No beating
around the bush, now. "I have to find Gary."

Chapter Four

Rand remembered the first time he'd seen a woman hold her newborn baby. It was when his own mother had Alicia. He'd been only fourteen at the time, still reeling from his stepfather's desertion and his sudden elevation to "man of the house." His mother, like Susan, had been without insurance, and she'd had her baby at the Coastal County Hospital, classified as an indigent.

Rand had sat in a grubby waiting room, taking care of the seven-year-old twins, feeling scared and lonely and thinking that having a baby was the worst thing that could happen to a woman. But after it was over, Rand had been invited for a brief visit to his mother's room and a peek at his new sister. He had never seen his mother smile like that.

Since that time, he'd seen all three of his sisters within minutes of delivering their children, and they all had that glowing, ethereal look about them the first time they held their babies. It was the only thing Rand had ever seen that struck him with awe.

Susan was no exception. They didn't let her hold

the baby for long. Because Penny was premature, they whisked her away to an isolette in the neonatal unit as a precaution. But during those few seconds when Susan held her child, she was the most beautiful woman in the world.

Rand wondered how it would feel to be a first-time father. Not that he'd ever know. Once upon a time he'd assumed a wife and family were somewhere in his distant future, but given his abysmal track record with women, he'd given up that fantasy.

It wasn't something he'd worried much about, especially lately. He figured he'd waited a long time to have his house all to himself, and he wouldn't give up his solitude easily. But for at least half a second, when he'd gazed on Susan and Penny, he'd yearned—*yearned*—to be part of a family, to be a father.

He'd come down to earth in a hurry when Susan had talked about finding Gary. It was ridiculous to think, for even a minute, that he had any proprietary relationship with Susan or her baby. They belonged to someone else—even if he was a jerk, even if he'd disappeared.

"So what do we do now?" Alicia asked. They were out in the hall, giving Susan some privacy while she cleaned up and dressed.

Rand shrugged. "I guess we go home. And I find another carpenter to finish the bookshelves or that room will still be a wreck when your wedding rolls around." Alicia was getting married in a few weeks at his house, and she wanted the whole house to be in perfect shape for the big event.

"I'm not worried about that," Alicia said surprising him. "What about Susan? She doesn't have anyone."

"She has Arnette, who appears to be a good friend."

Alicia shook her head. "She just seems so alone."

"We can't take up for every lonely person we meet. We got her safely to the hospital, I made sure her medical bills would be paid. At this point she might like some privacy."

Alicia didn't look convinced, but she agreed they should at least let her rest.

That was before Susan declared she wasn't staying in the hospital.

"The baby should stay here, of course," Rand heard her telling the nurse who'd come to take her to her room. "But I'm not sick. I've just had a baby, which is a perfectly natural event, not an illness, and I can recuperate at home just fine."

"And how are you planning to breast-feed the baby when you're fifty miles away?" Arnette argued. "Susan, you know I'm a big fan of home birth, but I'm also in favor of mothers and babies being together."

"But the doctor said Penny will be here several days," Susan objected.

"At least stay overnight," Arnette said soothingly. "You had a difficult labor, you're very weak, and it's the middle of the night. You're not ready for an hour in the car and climbing two flights of stairs to your apartment.''

Rand knew he should stay out of it. But he figured if Susan understood she didn't have to pay her hospital bill, she would be more reasonable. He went back into the room.

"Susan, if you're worried about the cost, don't. It's taken care of.''

She sat on the edge of the bed wearing a hospital-issue gown and robe, looking very pale. She just stared at him, her blue eyes seeming even larger than normal.

"I don't mind taking care of it," he continued when she didn't immediately seem grateful. "I can afford it.''

"That's not the point!'' she sputtered indignantly. She cast her gaze around the room, looking for someone to agree with her. Alicia, Arnette, and the nurse scurried for the door like rats abandoning a sinking ship. "It's not your responsibility," Susan continued. "You hardly know me!''

"I just spent fourteen hours with you, helping you bring a new life into the world," he said quietly. "How can you say I don't know you?''

"I don't want to have a debt to you the rest of my life,'' she retorted. "Don't get me wrong, I'm very grateful for everything you've done. But I have to draw the line at your paying my bill. I'm sure the hospital will work out payments.''

"The hospital wouldn't have admitted you if I

hadn't given them my credit card,'' he said gently. ''And you don't have to pay me back.''

She slumped back onto the bed. ''Okay, okay. I'll stay here one night. But I *will* pay you back.''

''If it will make you feel better.''

''Yes, it will. My daughter is not coming into this world as someone's burden.''

''She isn't a burden, and neither are you.'' He reached for her hand, then thought better of it and stopped himself. ''Once upon a time I needed help, and someone gave it to me. Now I'm passing it along to someone else. And someday, you'll do the same. Or maybe you already have.''

With that he turned and left the room.

ONCE UPON A TIME I needed help... That sentence ricocheted around Susan's head in her sleep, and all the next day, which she spent mostly gazing through the neonatal nursery window at tiny, helpless Penny.

When had Rand needed help? He seemed so strong, so capable, an unstoppable force. It was hard to imagine him needing anything, depending on outside sources for support of any kind.

Not money, obviously. He lived in that wonderful old house, practically a mansion.

What was his story? she wondered. And who had helped him?

Penny wiggled, and Susan stared, fascinated. Had any so entrancing creature ever been born? Of course she was red and wrinkled, and her head was still a bit squashed looking, something that had alarmed Susan the first time she'd seen Penny, until Arnette had re-assured her it was normal and would fix itself before long. She was still the most beautiful child ever conceived.

But beautiful or not, the child would need food and clothes and a roof over her head. Susan knew she'd not planned as well as she could have for the birth. She had bought a crib and some newborn clothes and diapers, but she hadn't set anything up, as she'd been planning to move it all to her new apartment right after she finished Rand's bookshelves—before Penny made an appearance.

She had only a few days to get everything ready. Which meant she had to get started now. Whether anyone agreed with her or not, she was going home today.

LATER THAT AFTERNOON, Susan lay on her couch, feeling overwhelmed and miserable, and regretting her decision to leave the hospital. Arnette had picked her up from the hospital and brought her home, but the short trip had completely exhausted her. Plus, she missed Penny. She'd already called the hospital twice to check on her. Luckily Susan had plenty of milk, so she'd left behind enough supply for quadruplets.

Her next task was to finish packing. She didn't have much, just those few baby things, her clothes, a few dishes and books, her tools and the rocking chair her father had made for her when she was born. The rest of the furniture, rugs, lamps and pictures—her father's things—had stayed with their house, which she'd sold to cover his medical bills. But the idea of moving even a few small items seemed overwhelming.

Where had all her energy gone?

With a resigned sigh, she got up, retrieved some flattened moving cartons from behind the refrigerator, and started filling them. If she just moved very slowly, she could do it.

She'd only finished one box when her doorbell rang. Grateful for any company, she went to the intercom and punched the button, swearing that even if it was an encyclopedia salesman, she would press him into service, packing boxes. Had she been crazy to think she could do this herself?

"Who's there?"

"It's Rand Barclay."

"And Clark Best," another voice piped in from the background.

Rand? Oh, Lord. As she buzzed them in, she didn't know how to feel. She couldn't ask either of them for help—they'd done so much already. Yet she felt a germ of excitement at seeing Rand again. Rand, Penny's surrogate father. He'd probably faint if he knew the extent of her fantasies. The way he'd fussed over Penny, anyone would have thought he *was* her father. And Susan had allowed herself to extend the fantasy—long after she'd needed it to survive the pain and fear of labor.

Pleased that she was at least wearing a dress, she opened the door to admit her two guests. "What are you doing here?" she blurted out.

"We brought your truck back," Clark said.

"Though of course you're under strict orders not to drive it, not for a month," Rand added.

"Yes, I know. Thank you."

Then Rand almost exploded. "Susan, what are you doing out of the hospital? I almost fainted when they told me you'd gone home."

"I'm fine."

"You're not. You're white as milk." He grabbed her arm and guided her toward the sofa. "Sit down before you fall down. Is anyone here taking care of you?" His eyes seemed to take in everything at once. Susan was a little bit embarrassed at the shabbiness of it all. Not that it wasn't a perfectly good apartment, but she hadn't done much to make it homey. She just hadn't felt like it. Maybe she didn't know how to. The home she'd shared with her father had been the same for as long as she could remember, and she'd never changed anything—not until she'd sold the furniture. She'd liked the comforting sameness of it.

Then there was Gary's apartment, which had seemed to her already a home just waiting for her to move in. She'd changed nothing there, either, leaving it just as she'd found it when Gary sublet it out from under her.

"My landlady, Mrs. Regis, checks up on me now and then. She's going to bring me my meals in for the next couple of days."

Rand's gaze had focused on the half-filled box she'd been working on. "What's all this?"

"I'm moving. I have to. I can't keep a baby here."

"I hope you don't mean you're packing these boxes yourself."

"Yes, a little at a time."

"Well, not anymore. You are under doctor's orders to lie on that couch and not move. You are not a horse that can be hooked back up to the plow a day after dropping a foal."

Clark just stood back, obviously suppressing a grin.

"I'm taking it easy!" she protested. But just the same, she did lie back on the couch. There seemed no stopping Rand, and she certainly was in no condition to. She let him flatten her like a steamroller. And being steamrolled had never felt so good.

She loved watching Rand work. He rolled up his shirtsleeves and dug in, gathering armloads of books and placing them gently inside her boxes, wrapping her dishes in newspaper as if they were priceless china. He even packed up her messy desk, carefully stacking her important papers and bills and receipts so nothing would get lost.

The job was done inside two hours, all but the final cleaning.

"Is this all you have?" Rand asked when he paused to survey the pitiful stack of boxes, the secondhand crib, the tiny suitcase of clothes for Penny, the starter box of diapers.

"Plus the tools in the shed downstairs," she said. "I was planning to buy a few more things for the new place. It's just that Penny's early appearance put a kink in my plans. I'll get caught up in no time."

Susan couldn't quite understand what Rand muttered under his breath, but it sounded suspiciously like, "Like hell."

"What? What's wrong with that?"

"How were you planning to move all this stuff, huh? Were you going to hoist these boxes and climb down two flights of stairs—"

"Of course not. Mrs. Regis was going to help me."

"That eighty-year-old lady I saw watering roses in the front yard?"

"And Arnette, but she has another delivery today and probably another one tonight if it's not false labor, but Friday she has clear." The day Penny would come home from the hospital, if all went well. Susan couldn't imagine how she would juggle a move *and* bringing a baby home from the hospital all in one day, but she was sure it would get done somehow.

Rand reached into his pocket, pulled out a set of keys, and tossed them to Clark. They were her keys, she realized. "Start loading up Susan's truck. I'll be down in a minute."

Now, this was too much. "Rand, wait. You can't—" But Clark was already out the door with the crib under one arm.

"Do you have a key to your new place?" Rand asked.

"Yes, but—"

"Any reason you can't go ahead and move today?"

She wanted to come up with one. "You can't just come in here and start making decisions for me!"

"Why not? You obviously haven't been making the greatest decisions for yourself."

His criticism hurt more than it should have. What did she care what Rand Barclay thought of her decisions? He was just a customer. The secret, surrogate father to her baby, but really just an acquaintance. Still, she cared.

"I've been doing all right," she said unconvincingly.

"All right? You're thirty years old, reasonably intelligent from what I can tell, attractive..." He paused, looking her over with complete thoroughness. "...very attractive."

She sat up abruptly, her face heating, and she could only hope she didn't turn red.

"You've got skills. Yet you're living—"

"All right, yes, I'm poor. I'm wiped out. I'm going through a challenging period in my life, but I'll pull it together. Lots of people are poor, and isn't it just typical that a rich doctor would point his finger and criticize?"

"I was going to say, you're living in a vacuum. The fact that you're, er, having a money crisis is a concern, too, but I'm more worried about the fact you are completely alone, almost nothing in the way of personal possessions. No ties. How did you let that happen?"

To her horror, Susan's eyes filled with hot, angry tears. He was right, he was so right. After her father's death, she'd shut down emotionally. She'd gone on a downhill slide, looking for security and fulfillment in all the wrong places. How had he figured that out about her? She was sure she hadn't revealed anything other than what was necessary.

He sat next to her on the sofa. "I don't want to criticize. I want to help." And he folded her into his arms. That was a surprise, but it was even more shocking to Susan that she let him. He was meddling in things he knew nothing about, and yet it felt so good to lean into his broad shoulders. His arms felt so secure around her. And for the first time in months, she felt safe.

"M-my father was sick for almost a year," she said, her voice barely above a whisper. "Friends have a way of disappearing when that happens, particularly when there are money problems, too. They stay away because they feel awkward. By the time Dad died, I had to sell off most of his things just to get out of debt. So that's what I did because I don't like debt."

"So you've told me."

"I never went out of my way to reestablish friendships. Instead I met Gary, and I wrapped myself up in him to the exclusion of everything else. I was determined to be the perfect girlfriend. I thought we would get married."

"And what about after he...when you were on your own again?"

"I spent a lot of time waiting for him to change his mind and come back, to at least call and check on me to see if I'd survived being dumped. I didn't have to work very much, because he'd left me some money—"

"Decent of him," Rand said dryly.

"—so I sat in this apartment watching TV, watching my stomach grow and waiting for the phone to ring. Other than working out at the gym every day— because Gary had bought the membership and I still had a few months left—I did nothing." She was so ashamed, now, of how she'd acted. To have put all her emotions and energy into one person was just stupid.

"But at some point you woke up."

"Yes, that was exactly it. It was like I woke up from a deep sleep. And I was putting my house back in order. I'd found a new apartment, made plans for a home birth with Arnette and got a few small jobs, including your bookcases. But making friends, building people into your life, that takes time. I'm just not there yet."

"But you were forging ahead, alone."

"What other choice did I have? I mean, you and Clark and Alicia—you've been wonderful. But I can't expect you to adopt me."

He stroked her hair. "Then why not have us as friends?"

What he was doing to her hormones did not feel like something a friend did. She suspected his touch was purely innocent on his part, but it sent her blood zinging through her veins. She tried not to think about it, tried to accept the comfort in the spirit with which it was given—the spirit of friendship.

"I'd like that. But friends don't order other friends

around and make all their decisions for them," she reminded him.

"Fair enough. Will you please let Clark and me move your things into your new apartment?"

"That would be most appreciated."

"And could I loan you a few baby things? I've got an attic full. You've got a nice crib, but you'll need a changing table and a chest of drawers and all that."

"That would be wonderful."

He kissed her on the forehead. "There, that wasn't so hard, was it?"

The feel of his lips on her forehead burned a permanent impression in her memory. She took a deep breath, clearing up the embarrassing tears once and for all. "It was, as a matter of fact. Gary said I was a clinging vine. He said I was too dependent, that I smothered him with all my love and attention, and that I expected too much from him and that I needed a life of my own. I don't want to ever be like that again."

"It sounds to me like you were on the ragged edge of clinical depression. He should have gotten you therapy. Instead he dumped you and sent you right over the edge."

"I know, but it's hard to see that when you're in the middle of it."

"You'll have to watch out for postpartum depression, too, since you apparently have the tendency."

"Nothing about having Penny could possibly make me depressed," she declared.

Rand smiled indulgently. "Spoken with the passion

only a new mother can produce. Can you say, '4:00 a.m. feedings'?''

WHEN RAND AND CLARK had finished loading Susan's thing into her truck, Rand helped her out to the landing, locked the door behind them, then lifted her into his arms and carried her down the two flights of stairs. She was lighter than he would have thought, and the sweet way she clung to his shoulders just about did him in, even as she groused that she could walk.

"Oh!" came a voice from the living room as they descended into the living room of the main house. "Isn't that romantic."

"Over the top, if you ask me," Susan grumbled. "I'm leaving now, Mrs. Regis."

Rand set her down, and the tiny, white-haired lady paused from watering her prodigious collection of African violets to give Susan a hug. "You don't have to rush off like this, you know. I would have helped you take care of the baby for a few days. How is she doing?"

"She's doing very well, thank you. I'll come back tomorrow and clean."

Rand just shook his head. She wouldn't, not if he had to come over here and scrub toilets himself.

"Don't worry about it, dear. I'll take care of it. Lord knows you have enough to occupy you."

After a few more tearful goodbyes, Rand managed to get Susan into her truck. He drove, and Clark drove Rand's Bronco, into which they'd packed a few boxes. Her scent teased him, just as it had when he'd carried her downstairs, and he had a hard time focusing on how to start the truck. He couldn't remember ever noticing a woman's scent in such a visceral way. Perfumes had always turned him off, but this was something lighter, like a sweet spring breeze.

"Where to?" he asked.

"Go out on 227 and head…north. It's just about… three miles." Her words were punctuated with snuffles.

"What's wrong?"

"I don't know. My hormones have gone crazy."

Rand didn't buy it. "I'm sure you can visit Mrs. Regis after you're settled in. Your new place isn't that far away, is it?"

"It's not that. It's Penny. I don't know how it's possible to get so attached to someone in such a short time…"

Rand gritted his teeth and turned the truck toward Savannah. He didn't really have time for another round trip to the hospital. He was getting farther and farther behind on his writing, and he still had some work to do at the lab. But mother-love was one of those irresistible forces he didn't dare challenge.

The only force that even compared, he figured, was sexual attraction, something near and dear to his heart at the moment. It didn't make sense. Susan had a pretty face, and she always smelled incredible, but her figure was not much to speak of at the moment, particularly in that tent dress she was wearing. She was all puffy and swollen from childbirth, she had dark circles of exhaustion under her eyes, and her hair was pulled back from her face in a no-nonsense braid.

What was it about her?

He'd been attracted to lots of women. He'd craved their bodies, taken them to bed and gotten over it.

This was the first time he had an overriding urge to be some woman's hero.

Chapter Five

Once Susan was with Penny again, a team of mules wasn't going to drag her away. The nurses at the hospital took pity on her and gave her a cot in a storage room near the neonatal unit.

Rand and Clark left her there. Rand figured they could get all her stuff moved in, adding a few things from his attic, while she was bonding with her baby.

Rand eyed the house with a critical eye when he pulled Susan's truck into the driveway of her new abode. It looked decent enough, a nice white brick house with shutters, and behind it, a detached three-car carriage house with an apartment on top, which was to be Susan's.

"It's not very big," he said to Clark.

"It'll be fine," Clark replied. "It's a nice neighborhood."

"I don't like the looks of that staircase that leads up to the front door."

"She's a carpenter. She'll fix it."

Rand climbed out of the truck just as a wiry little

man in work clothes came out the side door of the house to meet him.

Rand introduced himself. "I'm here with Susan Kilgore's things."

"Rex McKee." The man shook his hand, then nodded toward the truck. "That's fine, but I thought she weren't moving in till Friday."

"She had a slight complication."

"Yeah, a five-pound one," Clark added, coming to stand beside Rand. Rand elbowed him.

"I was planning to air out the place and clean the carpets afore she moved in," McKee explained. "But I guess if you've got the truck full of stuff, I'd better let you haul it on in."

"Thanks. We've got the key," Rand said. "We'll show ourselves up." He and Clark each grabbed a couple of boxes and headed up the stairs.

Rand frowned once he got the door open. The place was a bit grimmer than even her last apartment, and it did have a rather dank smell, but it appeared to have all the amenities—a working kitchen, circa 1950, a combined living/dining room with a bath to the side, and—

"Um, boss?" Clark said from the doorway that presumably led to the bedroom. "I think it's going to take some powerful carpet cleaning to get rid of this spot."

Rand went to the doorway and looked inside. The room was very bright. That was because there was a hole in the roof as big as his dining-room table, with a tree branch protruding through. The room was virtually filled with debris, the carpet soggy from recent rains.

"Well, she can't move in here," Rand said cheerfully.

Mr. McKee was a bit more distressed when they showed him the damage. "Musta happened the other night when we had that big storm. I had no idea. It'll take me a couple of weeks at least to fix things up. I'll return Miss Susan's deposit, if she wants."

"Why don't you hang on to it," Rand said. "Susan has a place to stay for the next few weeks. Just call me when the carriage house is ready. No hurry." He handed McKee a card.

Clark waited until they were alone to speak. "No hurry, huh?"

"Well, I don't want him to rush and do a shoddy job," Rand said.

Clark grinned. "My man. I knew your hormones would kick in where Susan was concerned."

"What are you talking about?"

"She's perfect for you. And with a ready-made family. Though I think if you're trying to make a play for her, you shouldn't order her around like you did earlier. Dierdre would slice and fricassee me if I did that to her."

Rand stuck Susan's truck key into the door lock and gave it a savage twist. "Where did you get the idea I'm trying to make a play for Susan?"

"A man doesn't usually invite his carpenter to be his houseguest, that's why—and I assume that's the plan—unless he has ulterior motives. I'm guessing yours are of a romantic nature. I've seen the way you look at her.''

"That is the most ridiculous thing I've ever heard. I'm doing a charitable thing, that's all. She's a woman with a baby who doesn't have a roof over her head. If I didn't let her stay with me, she'd be on the street.''

Clark just gave him a knowing look, then ambled over to Rand's Bronco. "Guess that book is going to take a little longer to get written,'' he called over his shoulder.

SUSAN SAT ON PINS AND needles as Penny underwent her final checkup before being released. She'd already gained a few ounces of weight, she was eating like a pig, her color was peaches and cream, and her blue eyes shone with bright interest.

Susan hadn't left the hospital for the past three days. She'd decided it was foolish of her to think she could stay away, even for a few hours.

The nurses had been very kind. It wasn't the first time a woman spent the night in that supply closet, they'd told her, nor would it be the last. She slept, and she nursed the baby, and stared at her in her is-olette, and then stared some more. She was feeling much better, especially since she'd gotten that crying business out of her system.

She was still a bit put out at Rand, too. Where did Rand come off, criticizing the way she conducted her life? He didn't have any concept of what she'd gone through the last few months. She'd been grieving.

Okay, maybe not in a very healthy way. She'd latched onto Gary in desperation, then focused all of her attention on him to distract herself from her grief.

But she'd merely delayed the process. After Gary left, she'd been forced to grieve for his loss as well as her father's, compounded by money worries and the stress of an unplanned pregnancy. It was a wonder she'd done as well as she had.

It might not be pretty at the moment, but it was her life, and she was in charge of it, and she resented the hell out of Rand and his power trips. Taking her to the hospital and staying with her during labor was one thing—that was kind and considerate. But paying her hospital bill? Deciding how and when she was going to move, then doing it for her? Ordering her to lie down, carrying her down stairs—it was ridiculous.

Maybe he meant well, but enough was enough. She intended to stay away from him.

The bookshelves were her last connection to him. She had a contract, she'd made a commitment, and she would not tarnish the name of the company her father had spent his whole life building. But she was done with anything more personal.

It wasn't that she didn't trust him. She didn't trust herself. She was in a delicate emotional state, just as she'd been when she met Gary, and she was all too susceptible to Rand's raw sexual appeal.

"You've got yourself a keeper," the pediatrician told her, handing Penny into Susan's arms. "Do you have a regular pediatrician, or would you like for me to keep seeing her? I have an office in Beaufort.'' He handed her a card.

"I'll take her to you," Susan decided firmly. She liked Dr. Bagley, and Beaufort wasn't a terrible drive. "Do you have an infant car seat?"

"Oh, my gosh, no. I forgot all about that."

"It's okay, we have some on hand to lend out. Just return it when you buy a replacement." He sent an orderly to get her the car seat, then disappeared.

Arnette met her in the business office, where she had to sign off on some papers. The final bill wasn't as staggering as she'd thought. "I want you to tear up Dr. Rand's credit card slip," she said bravely. "I'll make a down payment on this now, and I can pay two hundred dollars per month starting in November."

"Susan!" Arnette hissed. The midwife had again offered to take Susan and Penny home from the hospital. "Don't forget, you haven't paid *me* yet."

"You'll get paid. Everyone will get paid. I am not destitute." She wrote out a check to the hospital that almost wiped her out, but at least she had her first month's rent paid at the carriage house and all of her other bills up to date.

Arnette's beeper went off. She left to make a phone call while Susan signed papers. When she came back, she had an ominous look on her face.

"I have to deliver a baby here in Savannah. I can't take you and Penny home. But let me put you in a taxi."

"No, that'll cost a fortune. I'll call someone else."

Rand pulled up in his SUV less than a hour later. He must have dropped everything to come to her rescue. She regretted the unkind thoughts she'd had about him earlier. How could she stay mad at a guy who would fly to come to her aid like that?

She simply resolved to be more resistant to him in the future.

His car, which she'd paid little attention to when she was in labor, was the most luxurious vehicle she'd ever ridden in. It was just a Bronco, but it had every option imaginable, from temperature-controlled leather bucket seats to a built-in satellite guidance system. Penny slept peacefully in her borrowed car seat in the back, and Susan rode up front, giving the baby an anxious glance about every thirty seconds.

"She's not going to evaporate, you know."

"She's just so tiny, even though she's gained three whole ounces. And she seems so fragile."

"Yeah, but that kid's tough. Like her mom."

"You really think I'm tough?"

"Yes, I do. I want to apologize for the things I said the other day. You seem to be working things out just fine."

"How did the apartment look?" she asked. "Did Mr. McKee air it out and clean the carpets like he said he would?"

"Well, no, not exactly."

Susan winced at the thought of the smelly carpet. She would clean it herself, when she had more energy. Meanwhile, she wouldn't let Penny within five feet of it.

"Oh, you just missed my exit. I'm sorry, I should have been paying—"

"I missed it on purpose. I'm taking you back to my house."

She laughed, thinking he must be kidding. "You're kidnapping us?"

"Your apartment isn't livable, so I moved you into my guest room till you can make other arrangements."

Now he'd gone too far. "There was nothing wrong with that apartment! I know it was a little bit shabby, but—"

"A tree branch came through the bedroom roof. It'll take your landlord a few weeks to fix it. If you stay with me, you can still have the same apartment when the repairs are done. If not, you'll have to search for something else. And I figured you had better things to do than apartment hunt."

Oh, she hated that he was so reasonable. How could she argue with such a sensible set of circumstances? "I don't know what to say. This isn't at all what I had in mind."

"Sometimes life gets in the way of the best-laid plans," he reminded her. "But I've got room. It's no problem."

She digested her new, unexpected circumstances for a few moments, then finally spoke again. "Just one question."

"Shoot."

"Why? Why are you doing all this for me? I've been nothing but a colossal pain in the neck from the moment I went into labor. I've left your bookcases half done. I'm nobody to you.''

He glanced over at her, his expression decidedly guilty. "I don't know why I'm doing it. Maybe it's too much for a…a friend to take on. I just know that I want to." He paused, then added, "You *are* somebody."

That was enough for Susan, for now. She'd never been one to accept charity, but this time she was stuck. She had no other choice. Even if she thought Mr. Regis could stand Penny's crying, Mrs. Regis had a new renter moving in in a few days. A hotel was out of the question, and it would take time to get her deposit back from Mr. McKee. Unless she wanted to chance a homeless shelter or live in her truck, she was moving in with Rand Barclay.

RAND WAS GLAD HE'D won that battle. He hadn't been sure how Susan would take his high-handed gesture. He should have asked before moving her belongings into his home, and he was surprised she'd gone along with it. He'd fully expected Susan's pride to get in the way of this very sensible solution to her problem.

The fact she hadn't put up much of an argument spoke of her dire circumstances.

He parked in the garage and showed her inside. She held the sleeping Penny in a death grip—she didn't seem at all comfortable with the infant. He kept a hand at her elbow so she wouldn't trip.

"Do you want to put Penny down for a nap?"

"I…I guess so. She was on a schedule at the hospital, but they said I could relax that once I'm home and do it however is comfortable for the both of us.''

"Penny looks pretty comfortable just as she is.''

"I think that's because I'm walking. She seems to like movement.''

"Let's see how she likes her crib. It's upstairs.'' He reached for Susan, intending to scoop her up in his arms again. Looking forward to it, actually. But she held up a hand to ward him off.

"No, no, I can do this on my own. I hold Penny with one arm, like this, and grip the banister with the other. Neither of us will fall.''

Sure enough, neither of them did. Rand walked up the stairs behind them, ready to catch anything that seemed to be heading downward, just to be on the safe side. It also gave him a nice view of her hips, which even in the baggy dress he could see swaying side to side.

He'd admired her butt even when she was pregnant.

"I've put you in two connecting bedrooms with a bathroom between. If you leave both doors open, I think you'll be able to hear the baby all right. Or, if you want her closer at night, you can use the bassinet right in your room.''

"I don't have a bassi—'' She stopped short as Rand led her into the nursery and turned on the light.

It did look pretty good, he had to admit. Although Clark and Alicia had done most of the work, he was the one who'd decided Penny would have a proper room for herself. Clark had shined up Susan's crib and the beautifully carved rocking chair, then brought down some more-or-less matching furniture from the attic—a chest, a changing table, and a toy box brimming with plush animals.

Then Alicia had taken over. She'd made up the crib with a set of sheets featuring pink kittens and a pink blanket. She'd put all of the clothes Susan had bought into the chest of drawers, adding a few almost-new hand-me-downs from Betty's and Bonnie's girls. She'd hung a colorful mobile above the crib and a kitten wallpaper border just below the chair rail.

The final touch was a hand-hooked rug with kittens that she'd made herself as a craft project in high school.

"What do you think?" Rand finally asked when Susan still didn't say anything. "And don't say it's too much. Most of this stuff came right out of the attic."

"It's…it's absolutely beautiful. I'll have to take a picture of it, to show Penny when she's old enough. I just never imagined I would have anything this nice, at least not to start with."

"Alicia did most of this," he felt compelled to say.

"Well, she's a very sweet person. I'll call her later and thank her. But the rooms are in your house, so thank you, too." Her eyes shone, and Rand was sure she was going to kiss him on the cheek.

Penny chose that moment to wake up with a cranky sob, which quickly escalated into full-scale squalling.

Susan's smile of gratitude abruptly fled. "Oh, dear. Do you think she wants to eat already?"

"You're asking me?"

"It's too soon. Maybe she needs a new diaper." Susan glanced around, her gaze finally settling on the changing table. She headed for it, but stopped halfway there. "Diapers. The hospital gave me a little bag of things—"

"It's still in the car, I'm afraid. But the other ones you bought are in the top drawer of the changing table."

She opened the drawer and extracted one impossibly small diaper.

Rand watched, itching to dive in and help as Susan struggled with unsnapping Penny's pink cotton sleeper and removing the diaper, which was indeed wet. But every new mother had to figure it out for herself, he'd learned.

"Um, um…" Susan held out the soiled diaper, frowning at it like it was nuclear waste. Oh, boy. Wait till she encountered her first *really* dirty one.

"Trash pail is on your left. It has a foot pedal."

She tossed the offending diaper, looking relieved. "Wow, that's convenient."

She started to put the clean diaper on without using a baby wipe. Rand knew he shouldn't butt in, but he couldn't *stand* the thought of diaper rash. Occupational hazard. "You're probably looking for these." He shoved a package of wipes at her.

"Um, yes, of course."

The rest of the operation went smoothly, though Susan had to adjust the tape three times before the diaper would stay on Penny's tiny body. At last the baby quieted down, and Susan put her in the crib. Penny went right back to sleep.

"She's so little, I could fit ten of her in this crib," Susan said with a yawn.

"That won't last long. Your room's this way."

He practically had to drag her away from the sight of her sleeping child. New mothers were so funny.

Susan's eyes nearly popped out of her head when she saw her bedroom. For one thing, it was huge. For another, it was the most luxurious room she'd ever seen, with pale blue walls, snowy white trim and inch-thick carpeting and furniture that all matched. The bed, in particular, drew her attention. It seemed the size of a football field, but maybe that was because she'd been curled up on a lumpy cot all week. And the comforter looked like it could swallow two or three people.

"Alicia put your clothes in the closct."

Susan couldn't help herself. She opened the closet to see how her clothes would look here. Just as she'd suspected, pretty pitiful. No one had ever hung up her overalls before, particularly in a walk-in closet that was as big as her kitchen in her old apartment. She would have laughed if she hadn't been so completely exhausted.

She sat on the edge of the bed. "I feel like I'm staying in the Waldorf."

Rand laughed. "That would make me the concierge. Would madam like something to eat? Clark can probably rustle something up for you."

"What I'd really like is to sleep. I don't think I've

slept more than twenty minutes at a time this whole week.''

"Go ahead, then.''

"All right, but…'' She looked troubled all the sudden.

"What?''

"Can I leave the nursery door open? Will you listen for Penny, just in case I don't hear her? I'm usually a heavy sleeper.''

He gave her an indulgent smile. "Of course. But with the set of lungs that kid has, I don't think anybody in the house will sleep if she has a mind to wake them up.''

He left her alone, and Susan wasted no time shucking her clothes and sliding between the whisper-soft, flowered sheets. She didn't even bother with pajamas, wanting to thoroughly luxuriate in this overwhelmingly feminine environment. Gary's apartment had been nice, but very masculine. Everything had been brown or tan or beige.

Monochrome. Like her life had been.

As she drifted off to sleep, she thought about how much time she'd wasted waiting for Gary to change his mind. That time should have been used to better prepare for Penny's arrival. She'd thought she *was* prepared, until this week.

She awoke some time later to the sound of Penny crying. Instantly alert, she leaped out of bed, ran through the connecting bathroom and made it to the crib in about ten seconds.

"I'm here, Penny, don't cry.'' She picked up the

squalling infant and cuddled her, but that didn't stop the noise. According to the Winnie the Pooh clock, it was almost six. Susan had slept for almost two hours. That was a record. "All right, shh, hush now, it's dinnertime."

Like a pro, Penny latched onto Susan's breast and started feeding, her cries silenced like magic.

"That's a good girl," Susan crooned, heading for the rocking chair.

Rand appeared in the nursery doorway. "Is everything o—oh!" He turned bright red and backed away.

Just about then, Susan realized she was stark naked.

Chapter Six

"Um, I guess everything's okay, huh?" Rand called from the hallway.

"Yes, yes, everything's fine." *Except I'm dying of embarrassment.* "Thank you for checking."

"Dinner will be ready in about an hour," he added.

She reached out with her foot and nudged the door shut. It didn't go all the way, but Rand's hand grabbed the knob and pulled the door closed soundly.

This is never going to work, Susan thought, even as warm, maternal thoughts bubbled through her as a result of the nursing. She was used to living alone. She didn't even *own* a robe. She'd always just used one of Gary's shirts. For that matter, she didn't own any sort of lounge clothes she could wear in public. Not in this house, anyway. She just didn't think she could show up to Rand's dinner table in her ratty sweats.

Carrying the baby with her, she wandered into her own room and checked out the closet again. She had three very casual maternity dresses and her overalls. The rest of her clothes—and Gary had bought her some very nice things—would be way too small until she lost some weight.

Depressed, she selected one of the dresses, a pair of black tights, and her trusty black Birkenstocks. She did not want to go down for dinner. She did not want to face Rand again today, and maybe not in this lifetime.

But she didn't have a choice.

RAND SAT AT HIS DESK, the computer on, fingers tapping away at the keyboard. Notebooks and textbooks were spread out all over his desk for easy reference. He'd figured out how to use the footnote and bibliography features on his word-processing program. And to his utter surprise, he'd written the opening three pages of the introduction for his book.

The pages were more about him than anything—how he'd chosen his field of research, and how he'd become interested in dermatology. After all, most little boys didn't declare they wanted to grow up and study skin. Well, not in any *medical* way.

In tapping out those few, easy pages, he'd renewed his purpose in writing the book, fired up his interest. And all he'd really intended to do was take his mind off the way Susan Kilgore looked naked.

Like a Madonna. One without clothes.

Okay, enough, already.

"Well, what do we have here?"

Startled, Rand looked up to see Clark looming over him. "Must you sneak up on me that way?"

"I walked into this room same way I always do.

Only difference is, you're concentrating on something. For a change.''

Rand shook off his irritation. How could he be irritated when he'd written three whole pages? In only an hour, he realized, checking his watch. If he continued to work at that rate, twelve hours a day, he could make his deadline.

"Something smells good," Rand commented.

"Must be my new aftershave."

"I mean, dinner-wise."

"Oh, yeah. Red snapper sautéed in butter, wine and rosemary, with baby new potatoes and steamed broccoli. Cheddar-puff dinner rolls and tiramisu for dessert. And it's ready."

Rand's stomach rumbled in anticipation. "Have you called Susan?"

"She's already at the table."

Rand felt his panic returning. He wasn't ready to face her yet, but he supposed he better get it over with. "What's she wearing?"

"What?" Clark looked at him like he was crazy.

"Just tell me what she's wearing." And please, don't let it be anything sexy.

"A dress, I think."

"Okay. What kind of dress? It's not slinky or low-cut or anything, right?"

"Go sit down. I'll be right in with the rest of the food."

When Rand entered the dining room, he found Susan not only dressed, but looking pretty damn gorgeous. She was, in fact, wearing a denim dress, per-

fectly demure with long sleeves and a scoop neck.
But she'd done something with her hair. It was up, in
a twisty thing, kind of poufed out.

And she wore...makeup?

"Hi, Susan," he said with forced casualness as he
strode into the room and took his place at the head
of the table. "Did you have a nice nap?"

"Quite restful, thank you." She didn't meet his
gaze. "And quickly, before Clark gets back, I am so
sorry about...about..."

"No problem." Unless she made it a habit to walk
around the house naked. Then there would be one
helluva problem.

"Penny woke me up. I was sleeping so soundly,
then I heard her cry and I jumped up and ran in there
still half-asleep. I'm used to living alone. I just wasn't
thinking."

"Susan, it's okay. The trauma of seeing you naked
won't cripple me for the rest of my life. A couple of
years of therapy ought to take care of it."

She looked stricken rather than amused.

Clark entered the dining room just then, and Rand
had never been so grateful for the distraction of food.
Clark unloaded a heavily laden tray, putting dish after
dish onto the table. Then he filled everyone's plates
before taking his own chair.

"This smells incredible," Susan said before sam-
pling the fish. "Oh, my God, this is heaven. Don't
tell me you eat like this every night."

"Not every night," Rand said.

"I thought I'd do it up nice tonight," Clark said,

"seeing as how this is your first night with us and all."

"You don't have to treat me like an honored guest," Susan objected. "I think I'm more of a nuisance than anything. In fact, I'd like to pitch in with some of the cooking and cleaning—"

"Don't even think about it," Rand interrupted. "The kitchen is Clark's territory. No one's allowed to even touch his pots and pans. One time I tried to wash one of his skillets with the wrong kind of soap. He screeched at me like a fishwife."

"Oh." Susan focused on her food for a few minutes, pausing every so often to sigh appreciatively. Rand sighed every so often, too, but not because of the dinner. It was the view.

Now that he'd seen Susan naked, he couldn't help thinking about her that way.

"Well," Susan said, "at least I can continue working on your bookshelves while I'm here. Penny's still sleeping a lot—"

"Absolutely not," Rand said. "You're to rest and take it easy for at least a month. I don't want you lifting anything heavier than Penny."

"Well, I have to do something. I'm not cut out to be a lady of leisure. I found that out already."

Rand gave her concern some serious thought. He suspected she was prone to depression, and she was likely to get the blues if she didn't have something besides the baby to occupy her thoughts. She might also wile away her days mooning about Gary.

"Do you do kitchen cabinets?" Rand asked her.

"Sure."

"Why don't you and Clark put your heads together and redesign all of the kitchen storage? It needs updating, so Clark tells me."

"Well, all right, it's about time!" Clark said.

Susan perked right up. "I'd love to do that."

"And that fireplace mantel in the office—it's a nightmare. You can draw up plans for a new one of those. And the closet in the master bedroom could use some better shelves." He stopped there, pausing to think about Susan in his bedroom.

"The garage could use some storage," Clark added, getting into the spirit of things. "I know that's not fine woodworking like you're best at, but it still needs a carpenter."

"I can do that," Susan said. "I'm not exactly in a position to be picky about the jobs I take."

"Well, there you go," Rand said. "Do up some drawings, write up bids, whatever. And after your one-month checkup, if Arnette okays it, you can get to work then."

"Don't forget Alicia's wedding," Clark said.

"Oh, right. Everything has to be neat and clean for the wedding December first."

"I can work around that. This is great. How about if I give you a great big discount in return for my room and board?"

Rand started to refuse, but then he rethought the situation. Susan's pride again. She would feel better about everything if she believed she wasn't getting a free ride. And maybe, just maybe, she wouldn't bolt out the door the first chance she got.

"We'll work something out," he said.

DURING THE NEXT COUPLE OF WEEKS, Susan felt like she'd stepped into someone else's life. In some ways it was delightful. She never had to lift a finger for herself. Clark made almost all of her meals, and on those occasions when he was away at school or with his girlfriend, he always left something for Susan that could be quickly heated in the microwave. She'd never eaten so well, but to her surprise she was losing weight. Thank God. She'd never had to worry about that before.

In some ways those first few days in Rand's house were terrible, because she never got enough rest. Penny didn't seem to like sleeping very much. She wanted to be held and rocked and nursed almost all the time, and the rate at which Susan had to change the baby's diaper was staggering. She went through her starter box of diapers on the first day and had to ask Clark to get her some at the store. She wrote a check for them, but two days later the check still sat on the kitchen counter, uncashed.

And then there was Rand. He spent quite a bit of time at his job at Inman Labs, but whenever he was home, she could feel his presence, even if he was several rooms away. He made no special efforts to spend time with her, and she tried to stay out of his way, but they inevitably crossed paths.

Toward the end of the second week, she made a

fantastic discovery. Alicia, remembering all too clearly her first weeks with Dougy, brought over a clever device that allowed Susan to strap Penny to her back like a papoose. "Try this and see if Penny doesn't adore it," Alicia said, helping Susan adjust the straps. "At least your hands are free."

Penny did, in fact, adore it. So long as Susan kept moving, the baby was quiet. So Susan took her sketchbook and tape measure and went to the kitchen, baby on her back. She sat on a stool at the island and rocked back and forth as she sketched some ideas for how to revamp the kitchen cabinets.

That was how Rand found her when he came home from work that day.

"Good afternoon, Hiawatha."

"Hiya—oh." The papoose.

He set down his briefcase and opened the refrigerator, settling on a bottle of mineral water. "How was your day?"

"Oh, it was rousing. First, the Spanish Inquisition stopped in, but I told them you were at work. Ditto Ed McMahon. Then a Hollywood talent agent came looking for me, but I told him I was much too busy to accept that role starring with Tom Cruise."

Rand looked thoughtful. "I wasn't expecting the Spanish Inquisition today."

"No one expects the Spanish Inquisition."

"Was your day really that boring?" he asked on a more serious note.

"Oh, not bad, really, I'm just teasing. I fed Penny, I changed her. I put her down. I picked her up. I rocked her. I'm beginning to think she's an insomniac. But she went to sleep about an hour ago, finally, so I'm brainstorming ideas for your cabinets.''

"Sounds like you need a break. You haven't left the house since you got here."

Was he hinting around that maybe she ought to be working a little harder at finding a new home? Although she tried not to bother him, he must miss his privacy. She'd talked to Mr. McKee on an almost daily basis, and the repairs to the garage apartment were nowhere near done. There'd been a lot of rain lately, making roof work impossible.

"Nowhere to go, and no way to get there," she said with a regretful shrug. "I can't drive, remember?"

"Of course I remember. If I provided the place to go and the way to get there, and a baby-sitter, would you be interested?"

Susan tried not to do something totally embarrassing, like drop her jaw and gawk or sputter. Was...was Rand actually asking her *out*? Like, on a *date*?

"I, um, that really does sound nice, but I'm not sure I'm ready to leave Penny."

"Just for a couple of hours. You can use my cell phone and call in to check up on her. Anyway, you'll just be a couple of miles away. Okay, here's the deal. Alicia and John—that's her fiancé—want to check out this new restaurant as a possible location for their rehearsal dinner. Clark and Dierdre are going, too. And we all thought it would be nice if you joined the party.

"You're bound to be craving some adult company," he added. The way he said "adult company" sent a thrill down her spine. A totally inappropriate thrill, she reminded herself. There was still Gary. Not that she was counting on their getting back together. But Gary felt like unfinished business. She had to locate him and tell him about Penny. She was in limbo till she got that settled.

And that meant no girlish fantasies about the very nice, very handsome man who was currently playing white knight in her life.

"Who did you have in mind to baby-sit?" she asked.

"One of my other sisters, Betty. She has two daughters, so she knows the routine."

Susan was about to say yes when Rand added, "I'll be here, too, but I need to get some work done."

For the second time in as many minutes, Susan schooled her face so as not to reveal her true emotions. She felt like an idiot. Rand hadn't been asking her out on a date. What in the world would give her such a preposterous idea?

Now the dinner party didn't hold much appeal, but maybe it would be good for her. She'd hardly let anyone touch her daughter since she'd come home from the hospital. Susan supposed she'd been a bit proprietary about her, but weren't new mothers entitled?

She looked down at her clothes. She'd squeezed into her biggest pair of jeans this morning, but she'd only managed two buttons, covering up the situation with a sweatshirt that went halfway to her knees.

"I don't have anything to wear."

"It's a pretty casual place. One of your dresses will do just fine."

Susan mustered a smile. "Rand, I have one other problem. I can't really afford a nice dinner out."

"John's paying."

She'd run out of excuses. The truth was, she didn't want to go. She adored Clark and Alicia, and she would love to meet John and Dierdre, but if someone was willing to baby-sit for a few hours, she would just as soon use the time to sleep. Funny, but when she'd thought Rand was going, she'd have jumped through burning hoops to be included. Exhaustion was doing strange things to her brain.

There didn't seem to be a graceful way out of this.

"All right, I'll go, if they promise to get me back early."

"Shouldn't be a problem. They'll be here at seven."

That gave her plenty of time to get ready. "Well, thank you, it's very kind of you to think of me."

Upstairs a few minutes later, she went to her closet, again contemplating her pathetic wardrobe. On a whim, she dug through a box of her "skinny" clothes and came up with a short black skirt. She couldn't button it, but if she wore a long sweater over it, no one would know. She found a thin black one shot through with gold threads. That would do. She could dress it up with real stockings, high heels, and her mother's gold locket.

Maybe tonight would be fun after all.

She dressed with care, making sure she didn't run her last pair of nylons. That done, she sat down at the lighted vanity in her bathroom and did makeup and hair, Penny lying in her lap. Her traitorous imagination let her pretend she was dressing to go out with Gary. He hadn't taken her out very often, but when he did, he always wanted her to look her best. Susan suspected that was more for the benefit of his vanity than hers, though.

She imagined walking downstairs, Gary waiting for her in the formal living room. Only the face she saw wasn't Gary's, it was Rand's.

Darn it, she had to stop these childish fantasies about Rand! He'd made it perfectly clear he had no interest in her, except as a charity case. If he had, he'd be going to dinner with her instead of foisting her off on his friends and family.

She was ready early, so she dug around in her wallet for her only picture of Gary, a snapshot she'd taken with him looking macho in his hard hat, work shirt, and steel-toed boots, his blond hair gleaming in the sun.

She'd stared at Penny for hours on end, trying to see some piece of Gary in her face or her personality, but so far, nothing.

She took the snapshot and taped it to Penny's crib, where the baby could see it. If Gary couldn't be here in person, at least Penny would be able to see a facsimile.

At quarter to seven she checked herself in the full-length mirror, deciding she didn't look half bad. The old Susan was starting to shine through. She even managed a smile, and she realized she hadn't seen herself smile in months and months.

When she came downstairs, Alicia was just letting herself in the front door. "Oh, look at you! You're gorgeous."

"Hardly," Susan said with a laugh, "but at least presentable. You look nice yourself."

Alicia wore a white sheath dress with a short cashmere cardigan over it in a buttery yellow. With her short, sassy hair, she looked almost like a flapper.

"Thanks. I'm glad you decided to come with us."

"It was nice of you to include me. But your sister's not here yet."

"We have plenty of time. Clark and Dierdre are out there necking in the car. I don't suppose you convinced Rand to come."

Susan hadn't realized that was a possibility. "Ah, no."

Rand strode into the foyer, his face a thundercloud. "Betty can't baby-sit. She just called. Jessica has come down with some bug."

Disappointment warred with relief inside Susan. "I hope it's not serious."

"Just a little stomach thing," Rand said. "But I'm sure you don't want any germs around Penny."

"No." Susan looked wistfully at Alicia. "Well, another time. Darn, I was really looking forward to getting out, too."

"Then you should go," Alicia said. "Rand can watch Penny."

"Oh, I don't think—" Susan tried to object, but Alicia wasn't listening.

"He needs another excuse not to write his rash book. It's okay, right, Rand?"

Rand did not look pleased.

"No, I will not let you be pressured into baby-sitting," Susan said firmly. "You have work to do."

"But it's only for a couple of hours," Alicia wheedled. "C'mon, Rand, please?"

"You don't have to say yes," Susan said.

Rand sighed dramatically. "I suppose I can manage for a couple of hours."

"Then it's settled," Alicia said decisively. "Where is Penny, anyway?"

"Asleep in her crib, for a change."

"Can I go peek at her?" Alicia asked. "I won't wake her up, I promise."

Susan smiled. "Of course."

Alicia scurried off, leaving Rand and Susan alone.

"You look great, by the way," Rand said.

Susan felt her face heating and knew she was blushing to the roots of her hair. "Thank you. I don't get a chance to gussy up very often."

From upstairs Penny let out a short wail, like a warning siren, breaking the odd spell that had fallen between them.

"Oh, jeez, I hope Alicia didn't wake her up," Rand said, casting a worried glance up the stairs.

"You're positive you want to do this? You can change your mind."

"If I did, Alicia would never let me hear the end of it."

"Then I'll just run up and check on the baby one more time." She got away from Rand as quickly as she could. The way he looked at her sometimes made her skin prickle with awareness.

Alicia was coming out of the nursery just as Susan came in. "It's okay, she went right back to sleep," Alicia said.

"Good. I just want to check in one more time before we leave."

"You're almost as bad as I was. See you downstairs."

Penny was indeed sleeping peacefully, breathing in and out with reassuring regularity. Susan resisted the urge to touch her. "Please, please be good for Rand," she whispered. "I don't care if you keep me up all night, but let him get his work done."

The picture of Gary caught her eye. She pulled it off the crib and held it in her hand, wishing that somehow she could conjure him up. How could a man disappear so thoroughly?

"Oh, Gary," she murmured. "You really must know your daughter. I have to find you."

Her eyes teared up briefly, but she knew it was just her hormones in revolt.

Someone tapped softly on the nursery door.

She quickly wiped her eyes and hoped she hadn't smeared her makeup too terribly. "Come in." She stuck Gary's picture back on the crib.

Rand opened the door. "You'll have to learn to be away from her eventually."

"But she's so tiny. Couldn't I wait till she goes away to college?"

"Everybody's downstairs waiting for you."

"You know where all my emergency phone numbers are?"

"Yes."

"And you said something about letting me borrow your cell phone?"

"Right here." He handed her a slim red phone no bigger than a compact.

"You promise you'll call me at the restaurant if there's any problem, no matter how small?"

"Yes."

Susan made herself go. It did feel good to get out of the house, but Penny was never far from her mind. Nor Rand. The restaurant was cozy and charming, dinner was delicious, the company wonderful. She found herself laughing, the sound alien to her ears. But she'd have traded it all in a heartbeat for her sweatpants, a dirty diaper and a squalling infant.

And Rand.

She supposed she was turning into an all-right mother after all, but her craving for Rand's company was a little harder to defend.

RAND ALMOST WISHED Penny would wake up and cry. Anything to distract him from his thoughts, which were decidedly inappropriate. When he'd seen Susan in that short skirt, her generous breasts delineated so perfectly by a tissue-thin sweater, his eyes had almost popped out of his head. He'd known Susan had a natural beauty about her. But he'd never guessed exactly how dazzling and glamorous she could be.

A delicate necklace had accentuated her long, graceful neck. And she had a pair of legs any Rockette would envy.

At that moment, he'd wished with all his heart that he was going out to dinner with the gang that night, that Susan would be on his arm. But earlier he'd ruled out Clark's broad hints that he take Susan as his date.

Susan was still in love with Gary. He'd suspected it before, but when he'd caught her crying over the guy's picture, that confirmed it.

He'd come to a decision. He knew an ace private investigator who could find anyone. Rand would call him this evening and sic him on Gary. Bringing the jerk back into Susan's life went against his better judgment, but it was better than watching her pine away, probably idealizing her memories of Gary.

Personally, Rand thought the guy sounded like a bad proposition, not very responsible, not very nice, and lousy father material. But Gary was what Susan wanted. And by God, Rand was going to get him for her. There was more than one way to be a hero.

Chapter Seven

Susan arrived home at a little before ten, her eyes drooping. She couldn't remember the last time she'd had an evening out, which meant she was out of practice—and it showed. Those few hours had exhausted her. She wondered idly what had happened to that girl she used to be who could stay out partying with her friends till all hours, then get up for an eight o'clock job with her dad.

She found Rand in his office—his very messy, disorganized office, she was ashamed to be reminded. She wished she'd been able to finish his bookshelves before Penny came along. He really did need more room.

He looked up from his desk. "Oh. You're home."

"Yes. Did you get much work done?"

"A couple of paragraphs."

She winced. "Penny was that bad? I don't hear her now."

Rand turned slightly, revealing the papoose on his back. "She started squalling about thirty minutes after you left. I searched all over for this papoose gizmo. Found it about ten minutes ago.''

With a sigh, Susan came forward to relieve poor Rand of his burden. ''Penny, you naughty girl, you're supposed to be good for D-D-D...Uncle Rand.'' Oh, my God. She'd almost called him ''Daddy.'' Was she going *delusional?*

Okay, she was sleep-deprived, but did that mean she had to carry her adolescent fantasies into real life? If she weren't careful, Rand would be calling in a team of psychiatrists.

She studied him as he typed a few words on his computer. If he'd caught her slip-up, he gave no indication.

''Did you have a nice time?'' Rand asked.

''Wonderful. The restaurant was beautiful, the food was first-class—not as good as Clark's, but delicious—and the company quite entertaining. It's nice to see couples so happy and in love.''

''Gets a little sickening sometimes, though, doesn't it? All that lovey-dovey-ness?''

''Not at all. I found it sweet.''

''Well, I guess if anybody deserves that kind of happiness, Alicia and Clark do. With their respective partners, I mean. They've both been through a lot.''

Susan had to agree. She'd gleaned a little more about her newfound friends this evening. Clark had been a promising professional football player for the Miami Dolphins when he blew out his knee his rookie year. For the next several years he'd succumbed to a prescription drug addiction.

He'd been in a bad way when Rand, one of his oldest friends, had found him and gotten him into rehab. Encouraged to explore new interests, he'd discovered he loved cooking. Rand had offered him a job and helped him get into the prestigious Culinary Institute. That was two years ago.

As for Alicia, she was only twenty-one. She'd gotten pregnant during college, forcing her to drop out. The baby's father had been no help. Rand had come to the rescue again, not batting an eye when Alicia moved back home, paying all of her bills and helping her get back on her feet again.

Rand had even introduced both Clark and Alicia to their respective fiancés. In fact, Susan had been a little worried her dinner companions were going to canonize Rand right there at the table.

"It sounds to me like you've taken care of everybody the last few of years," she said to Rand now.

"We're family. We take care of each other."

That sounded really nice to Susan. After her mother died when she was ten, she and her dad had always taken care of each other. She'd missed that most of all—caring for someone, worrying about them and having them do the same for her. No wonder she'd gone so overboard with Gary.

She had someone to care for and worry about now—Penny. But the other part of the equation was missing. She supposed that was why it had felt so nice for her new friends to make such an effort to include her in their evening out. No one had put her welfare first in a very long time, especially not Gary.

He was the type who never called to let her know he'd be late, never offered to do the dishes and he'd forgotten her birthday.

She hoped he wouldn't be so neglectful with Penny.

She was about to say goodnight when she spotted a stack of handwritten notes next to Rand's computer. They were damp and smeared beyond all recognition. "What happened there?" She pointed to the notes.

"Leaky diaper."

"Penny did that?" Susan was horrified. "Oh, my Lord, can you duplicate the notes?"

"Eventually. I know what books they came out of. I'll just have to get them back out of the library—"

"I'll help you. I'll go to the library tomorrow."

"Don't worry about it," he said gruffly. "It's no big deal."

Oh, but it was a big deal. She and Penny were proving themselves to be damned inconvenient. They were a two-girl wrecking crew, taking whacks at Rand's whole life. If she kept him from getting his book written, she would never forgive herself.

"Can't I do something to help?" she asked again.

"Just...just...no. Everything's under control."

And Susan recognized barely controlled frustration ready to rip out of its moorings. Her best move would be to just get out of Rand's face.

"Well, I guess I'll turn in," Susan said with a yawn, absently rocking Penny. "I really, really appreciate what you did tonight, Rand. It meant a lot to me. I have to confess I didn't want to go, but once I got there, I had a great time. I needed a few hours away from Penny.''

"I know. I've been around new mothers enough to recognize the signs. There are lots of baby-sitters available if you need them. My sisters will crawl all over each other to take care of a little baby. And Clark's pretty good in a pinch, too."

Susan heard what he didn't say—that no way in hell was she to ask *him* again. She wouldn't.

"Thanks for the tip. Good night." She got out of there before she did something really dumb, like burst into tears for no good reason.

RAND PUTTERED AT THE computer a while longer, thinking now that he was free of his baby-sitting duties he could really get some work done. But his productivity level didn't improve one iota. He wrote a few more paragraphs, but it was like pulling his fingernails out one by one to get those few pathetic words on the screen. He erased all but one paragraph, then shut down his computer. It was almost one in the morning.

He knew exactly why he couldn't write. It was too quiet, and his thoughts were haunted by images of Susan. She'd looked damn fetching in that sweater. And those black stockings... Rand broke out in a sweat at the memory.

He had to pass Susan's rooms to get to his, and he was surprised to see light coming out from under the nursery door. This was unusual, since Susan always brought the baby into her own room for the night, putting her to sleep in the bassinet. A light was on in Susan's bedroom, too.

Feeling a slight uneasiness that something might be wrong, he tapped lightly on the nursery door. "Susan?" he called softly. "Is everything okay?"

No response.

He knocked on the bedroom door, a bit louder, but still couldn't raise anyone. Returning to the nursery, he tapped again, then opened the door a crack, remembering far too vividly the last time he'd opened this door and entered uninvited. He wouldn't make *that* mistake again.

"Susan?" He peeked inside and saw her then, sitting in the rocker fully clothed. Or rather, almost fully clothed. Her sweater was rucked up on one side, where she'd obviously been nursing, but the thin black fabric had fallen back down when dinner was done.

Both Susan and Penny were soundly asleep, though even in a deep sleep, Susan held her baby protectively against her.

Relieved, Rand shook his head. Poor girl. She was so exhausted, she probably could have gone to sleep standing up. He couldn't leave her that way. She hadn't even taken off her high heels.

Wrestling Penny from Susan's loose grip was easy enough. He settled the baby into her bassinet, and she didn't stir at all. Rand watched her sleep for a few moments. He would never admit it to a living soul, but there was something about babies that really got to him. He'd been in hog heaven this evening, taking over Penny's care. The baby girl was creeping under his skin.

And so was her mother.

When he returned to the nursery, he noticed the snapshot stuck to Penny's crib and recognized it as the one Susan was crying over earlier—Gary, Penny's father. He felt an almost uncontrollable urge to seize the photo and rip it into a thousand shreds. The animosity he felt toward the man who had abandoned Susan and their child was palpable. He didn't even know the jerk, but if he ever met him, he'd be hard-pressed not to punch him out.

He could only hope fatherhood would force Gary to straighten up, if and when he was found. Some guys just took longer to grow up than others. He shook off his anger and turned his attention to the matter at hand—Susan.

What to do with her? He didn't want to wake her. Lord knew she got little enough peaceful sleep, and it seemed a sin to disturb her. But he couldn't leave her like that. She'd have a killer crick in her neck if she didn't already.

He decided to try to put her to bed.

Rand slid one hand behind her back and the other under her knees and gently lifted her. She showed no signs of waking.

She'd lost weight, he realized. Her waistline had reappeared. Judging from her arms and legs, he suspected she was naturally slender, and she was well on the way to regaining that state.

Unlike the last time he'd carried her, she was soft

and relaxed against him, her head lolling against his shoulder, her face partially curtained by her thick, midnight hair. His heart ached for her, looking so sweet and vulnerable in sleep. Other parts of him ached, too. It was going to be difficult to put her down.

He carried her out into the hallway, then through her bedroom door. Her room looked almost as if no one lived there. She kept it military-neat, and she had few personal possessions—almost as if she were afraid to get too comfortable in his home.

As he started to lay her down on top of the comforter, her arms slid around his neck in a reflex action.

"No, don' go," she said in a sleepy voice.

He almost dropped her. Oh, hell, this wasn't supposed to happen. "Time for beddy-bye, Susan."

Her grip on him tightened. "Only if you come, too," she said with a low, wicked chuckle. As he put her down, almost in a panic, she gave him a hard tug. Before he knew what had happened, he was sprawled on top of her, and she was kissing the daylights out of him.

At first he was just too shocked to move. Then his body responded in a big way. Without conscious decision, he kissed her back, reveling in the feel of her warm, moist mouth against his, her soft breath against his cheek, her full breasts pillowed against his chest. He was distressingly aware of every place their bodies touched, her weight on his arm, the way her hands trapped him gently against her, resting easily now on his back.

He had to stop this insanity, he realized. The woman was asleep, and he was taking unfair advantage of her vulnerable state, never mind she was the one who'd practically put him in a headlock.

It took all of his willpower, but he managed to break the kiss. With a bit more effort, he disentangled himself from Susan's sleepy embrace and pulled away, gasping for breath as if he'd just sprinted up and down the stairs ten times.

Abruptly Susan's eyes flew open. Confused at first, she took in the room, then him. Confusion changed to apprehension. "Did I...did we..." She put her hand over her mouth, looking horrified.

"I can explain," Rand said quickly. At least, he thought he could. But would Susan believe him if he told her she'd wrestled him onto the bed and assaulted him?

She looked away miserably. "No, there's no need. I'm so sorry, Rand. I guess I was dreaming. I must have thought you were Gary."

Rand started pacing. "No, I'm sorry. I wasn't exactly a victim, here. It was obvious you were acting in your sleep. I should have been a little more... resistant." He inched toward the door with escape in mind, denying the powerful urge to take her in his arms again, to soothe those lines of worry from her forehead. She thought she'd done something wrong?

She pulled a pillow over her face, muffling her next

words. "You must really think I'm pathetic, clinging so desperately to the memory of a man who's so completely out of my life."

"I think nothing of the kind. In fact, I think you're gorgeous and sexy and a very good kisser, and I'm really disappointed to know it wasn't me you were kissing."

Had he really just said that?

She said something else into the pillow, but he didn't quite catch it.

"What?"

She threw the pillow aside. "Nothing, nothing. Maybe we'd better just forget this ever happened, okay?"

Not in a million years. "Okay. Good night, Susan." He forced himself to turn and walk out, closing the door securely behind him.

Lord, he'd certainly not bargained for this when he'd invited Susan into his home. He wasn't the romantic type. He didn't fall for destitute waifs with babies in tow. He enjoyed seeing his friends and relatives find their perfect soul mates and fall in love, but he'd always been relieved to know that wasn't his fate. He just didn't relate to women on that deep, elemental level that led to fairy-tale romance.

Now, for the first time in his life, he'd found a woman with whom he had that potential. Strangely enough, he wanted to open up to her. He wanted her to know all his secrets, and he wanted her to share everything with him, as well.

And, damn his luck, the lady was in love with someone else.

SUSAN STARED AT THE DOOR long after Rand had disappeared through it, no longer at all sleepy. How could she have humiliated herself so thoroughly? Granted, she'd been asleep when the kiss started, but she was in no doubt as to how it had happened. She'd initiated it. She'd been dreaming something sexy, and there was Rand, and she'd just fit him neatly into her dream.

The line she'd tossed out about Gary, however, was only to save face. She hadn't been dreaming about Gary.

She finally managed to fall asleep again, and miracle of miracles, Penny didn't wake her up until seven. The baby had slept almost six whole hours! When they both woke up again, it was almost eight, and Susan felt better rested than she had in a long while. What a joyful day it would be when Penny slept through the night.

The house was deserted, so Susan made herself a bowl of cereal, then carefully cleaned up the mess so Clark would have nothing to complain about.

Feeling more optimistic than she had in a while, she got out her work materials and started a shopping list for the items she would need for Rand's new kitchen cabinets. It was an ambitious job, requiring strength and stamina, but she was confident she could take it on, even if she ended up hiring a muscular assistant.

The phone rang when she was in the middle of her calculations. She hadn't planned to answer it until she heard a male voice leaving a message for her.

She lunged for the phone. "Yes, it's me, this is Susan Kilgore."

"This is Rex McKee. I'm calling about the carriage house."

"Is it ready?" She certainly hoped so. The sooner she got out from under Rand's roof, the better.

"No, not exactly. See, the repairs are more extensive than I thought, and I can't afford to hire someone to do it. I'll have to do it myself, when I have time, and, well, under the circumstances, I think I better just return your deposit."

It took a moment for the man's words to sink in. "You mean I can't live in your apartment?"

"Not unless you're willing to wait several months."

She sighed. This was all she needed. "No, I'm afraid I can't wait that long. You can put the deposit in the mail to me." She rattled off Rand's address.

Now what? she thought after concluding her business with Mr. McKee. It had taken her forever to find an apartment she could afford that wasn't some rat hole. Now she would have to start the search all over again.

Determinedly, she located the newspaper, which Rand usually read early in the morning. It was in his office. She read through the "For Rent" section of the classifieds and got on the phone. After a couple of hours, she had appointments to see four properties this afternoon.

Now, her only problem was transportation. She called Arnette and left a message with her answering service, but the midwife was so busy lately Susan doubted she would have time to play taxi driver.

Next she called Alicia, but Rand's sister had a job interview that afternoon. "I'm really sorry," she said. "Can't Rand take you?"

"I haven't asked him, but I'm sure he has more important things to do. And Clark has classes this afternoon."

"Darn. Hey, I know, call Bonnie. She'd probably like an excuse to get out of the house, even if she has to drag the two kids with her."

"Alicia, I don't even know your sister."

"That's okay, she's really nice." Alicia gave her Bonnie's number, and Susan was just desperate enough to use it. But as it turned out, Bonnie, who did sound very nice on the phone, said she was caring for several other children that day as part of a baby-sitting cooperative she belonged to.

Out of options, Susan decided she would try driving herself. She wasn't supposed to get behind the wheel yet, but she felt pretty good, and she wouldn't be going terribly far. Marlena wasn't a large town, after all, although one of the apartments was in nearby Bainesville.

After lunch, Susan changed into jeans and her nicest sweatshirt, a forest green one with a seagull on it. She dressed Penny in her cutest, ruffliest outfit, hoping the two of them would make a nice impression on potential landlords.

She gathered up her keys, her purse, Penny's car seat, another gift from the Barclay's attic, to replace the one borrowed from the hospital, and headed out the back door. She was just unlocking the door to her truck, parked on the grass next to Rand's driveway, when Rand drove up.

He practically leaped out of his SUV and tromped over to her. "What in the hell do you think you're doing?"

"I've got to go look at some apartments," Susan explained, giving him all the painstaking details of her current dilemma.

"You couldn't have waited a couple of hours for me to get home? Hell, you could have called me at the lab."

"It didn't seem important enough to bother you. Anyway, I feel fine. I'm sure I'm up to driving."

"No way. It's been nowhere near a month."

"It's been almost three weeks." She didn't want to stand here and have this argument with him. She was going to be late to her first appointment. She opened the truck door, but instead of arguing, Rand calmly picked up Penny and her car seat and lugged them to his vehicle.

"Just where do you think you're going with my baby?" Susan demanded.

"I'll take you wherever you need to go. And you should think about buying another truck, one with a back seat. It's not safe for babies to ride in front, even in an approved car seat.''

Well, that stopped her. She hadn't even thought of that. As if she could just magically come up with the money for a new set of wheels.

''Don't you have a book to write?'' she said crossly, but she went along with his plans for her. This was one argument she wasn't going to win.

He waved away her concern. ''I've put it off this long. What's one more afternoon?''

Chapter Eight

Rand and Susan sat mostly in silence on the drive to the first apartment, with only Penny's happy gurgling to listen to. Susan didn't know whether to be miffed at his high-handedness or grateful. It was generous of him to give up his afternoon, even if it was done grudgingly, and he was right in advising her not to drive. The luxurious Bronco gave a much smoother ride than her old truck, and she would have had to wrestle with the sticky gear shift. She might've set back her healing by several days.

The first apartment was not in the choicest neighborhood. It was a fourplex in a hundred-year-old building close to downtown, and Susan had been intrigued by the ad, which mentioned that the building was on the historic register. But that distinction didn't change the fact that it was seedy. Outside the bricks were in desperate need of tuck-pointing, and several summers' worth of sun had blistered and peeled the trim paint.

"Maybe we should just skip this one," Rand said.

"No, now, it might be nicer inside. We've come

all this way, let's just give it a peek." She retrieved the baby from her car seat, and they went in search of the landlady, Mrs. Kim. The shirtless old man sitting on his downstairs patio smoking a cigar did little to enhance the building's image. Susan wondered if he even felt the cold.

Mrs. Kim was sweet, though, and she chattered anxiously as she led them upstairs to the vacant unit. Susan tried to build up some optimism, but that was quickly dashed when she saw inside the apartment. It was large enough, with spacious rooms and high ceilings, but the atmosphere was dank and cheerless. The kitchen was little more than a closet with a hot plate, and there were no laundry facilities on the property.

"The laundromat is around the corner, two blocks," Mrs. Kim said brightly.

Rand looked at her, frowning and shaking his head. "If it was just you, maybe, but can you imagine dragging your laundry around with a baby in tow?"

"I'm sure people do it all the time," Susan replied.

But Rand was right. And even without the laundry shortcoming, it would take massive rehabbing to make this place marginally livable. She thanked the disappointed Mrs. Kim, and they headed off for their next destination.

The second apartment was billed as "the servant's quarters of a large estate," which gave Susan hope. But the classified ad had exaggerated a bit. The servant's quarters turned out to be two bedrooms on the second floor of a not-very-big house. But at least there was a washer and dryer available for Susan's use, and she could store her woodworking things in a portion of the garage.

She thought it had possibilities, until Rand pointed out the obvious flaw. "Susan, the kitchen is in the *bathroom.*"

Technically he was right. The owners had taken what was once a huge bathroom, substituted a tiny prefab shower for the tub, put up a pressboard wall, and wedged in a minuscule refrigerator and stove.

"There's a wall between them," she said.

"It's not healthy," he insisted under his breath, so the landlady couldn't hear him. "I'm not even sure it's legal. I don't see any smoke alarms, a Girl Scout could pick the lock on the front door and I don't like the looks of that kid who lives here."

He meant the landlady's nineteen-year-old son, who had more piercings than a pie safe. He also smelled faintly of marijuana.

Susan realized she would have to cross this apartment off her list, too. She would not raise Penny anywhere near an illegal drug user, even for a short time.

It was the same with the other two. They weren't just disappointing, they were unworkable. Rand always pointed out some possible risk to Penny's health and well-being, and Susan immediately eliminated the place from the running.

After the last one, she climbed into Rand's car, feeling glum and pessimistic. She would have to consider some other arrangement—maybe sharing a house with another single mother. Maybe she could run her own classified ad under "Situation Wanted."

"Hey, come on, it's not that bad," Rand said. "You don't have to be in such a rush to find another place. It's not that terrible living with me, is it?"

Oh, how did she tell him? It wasn't terrible, it was wonderful—too wonderful. A girl could get spoiled really quick sleeping in that luxurious guest room, eating Clark's gourmet food. Most especially, a girl could get spoiled having someone like Rand worry about her.

Put her to bed.

Kiss her.

She'd managed to forget about the stupid kiss for a little while, but now she remembered it in all its gory detail.

"I just...I really need to get permanently settled some place," she said. "I need a home."

RAND DIDN'T REPLY TO THAT. Of course Susan needed to get her affairs settled. Though he'd taken great pains to make her feel welcome in his home, he knew how awkward it was to be someone's long-term houseguest. He'd lived with Clark's family for almost eighteen months when he was in high school. Mrs. Best's generous gesture of opening her home to him had probably saved him from a life on the streets. His own mother had fared much better without his stomach to fill.

But he remembered how he'd yearned for independence. Getting a scholarship to Georgia Tech had helped him achieve that.

Susan didn't have any scholarships coming her

way. In fact, she had some tough months ahead of her as she adjusted to motherhood while simultaneously rebuilding her finances and her business. She would just have to be patient about this moving-out business.

WHEN RAND PULLED INTO THE driveway and stopped in front, the door to the house opened and two small tornadoes whirled out. Susan realized they were children, and they attached themselves to Rand the moment he stepped out of the car.

"Unca Rand! Unca Rand!" they screamed in unison, hopping up and down. Rand, looking every inch the aggrieved but tolerant uncle, lifted the smaller child, a girl, into his arms and grasped the hand of the older one, a boy.

A woman came out the door next, and Susan had no trouble linking her to Rand's DNA. She had his dark hair, straight nose and square jaw, though her features were softer. It had to be Bonnie, Susan decided, because Alicia had told her that Betty's children were both girls.

Rand's sister smiled as she walked out to greet them. "Did you forget we were coming to dinner tonight?" Her gaze settled on Susan and her smile widened. "Hi, I'm Bonnie Deleva, Rand's sister. You must be Susan. Oh, and look at this cute girl. May I?"

"Be my guest." Frankly, Susan was exhausted from lugging around her six-plus-pound bundle. Susan turned the car seat so Bonnie could unfasten the buckle and pick Penny up.

"Come to Aunt Bonnie, precious girl."

Rand rolled his eyes. "Don't mind her, she's crazy for babies—anybody's babies—and she's everybody's Aunt Bonnie."

"It's been a long time since I held one this little," Bonnie said almost reverently. "She's darling."

"Thanks," Susan said, beaming with maternal pride.

"In answer to your question, no, I hadn't forgotten about dinner," Rand said. "I just had to make an unscheduled errand."

"My fault," Susan said. "Hope you haven't been waiting too long."

"No problem."

"Uncle Rand, can I look at those gross pictures again?" the little boy asked.

"Rand!" Bonnie scolded as they all went inside. "What gross pictures have you been showing my children?"

"Just some molds and fungi from a textbook."

"You're warping their little brains."

"I'm trying to instill a love of science in them. Hey, maybe one of your kids will grow up and discover a cure for cancer."

"Can I see the book, please?" the boy asked again.

"I'm afraid that book went back to the medical library, Shane," Rand replied, sounding almost relieved. "Anyway, I'm going to be very busy tonight."

Ordinarily, Susan would have intervened and cajoled Rand into spending a few minutes with his nephew. Children grew up too fast. Before he knew it, Shane would be more interested in computer games and cars and girls, and hanging out with his uncle wouldn't be a priority. But she'd already wasted so much of Rand's time today. She should do what she could to preserve what was left of the day for his writing.

"How about some pictures of bugs and viruses instead?" Susan suggested. "I bet Uncle Rand would let us borrow his new electron microscope pictures. They're really gross."

"What's a 'lectron mi-scope?" Shane wanted to know.

"Trust me, you'll like the pictures," Rand said. "Tell you what, we can look at pictures for fifteen minutes before dinner. Then I have work to do, so it's all kids out of the office."

"What office?" Shane asked.

"What used to be the playroom," Bonnie said. "And since when are you actually working at home?"

"No, he really is," Susan said. "He was supposed to get some work done this afternoon, but he took me apartment hunting instead." She wasn't sure why she felt compelled to defend Rand's work ethic.

"You mean you're moving out already?" Bonnie asked. "You just got here. Rand won't know how to act without some female with kids under his roof."

"Maybe I'll get some work done for a change," Rand groused. "Not that I'm hinting, Susan."

Too late. Of course he was hinting. He was as uncomfortable with the situation as she.

"Maybe us moms and kids should go in the backyard and play a game before dinner," Susan suggested, hoping to give Rand at least a few minutes of peace and quiet.

"No, no," Rand objected. "I promised Shane some bug pictures."

Shane looked at his mother. "Can we play croquet?"

Ah, the fickleness of youth. "Sure we can," Susan said enthusiastically. "I saw the croquet set on the patio."

"Yea!" The kids headed for the back door at full throttle.

Susan nodded at Rand, satisfied she'd done her part. "Your rashes are calling."

"Yeah," Bonnie agreed, "I think we can keep them quiet and occupied until dinner, anyway."

"Thanks," Rand said, not looking that pleased as he turned toward his office.

"Is he really writing?" Bonnie asked as they followed her children. "He's been procrastinating on this project for months. He claimed he'd really devote himself to it after Alicia and Dougy moved out, but it just made him grumpier, not more productive."

"No, he really is writing. A little bit, anyway. But I'm afraid my unexpected presence is ruining everything."

Bonnie shook her head. "Don't sweat it. Rand wouldn't know what to do if he didn't have some handy distraction as an excuse for why he's not getting his book finished."

Susan pondered Bonnie's observation as she helped the kids put up wickets for croquet in the lush backyard, which was still green despite the fact Halloween had come and gone. She was pretty sure she wasn't an excuse. She was a real distraction, and if not for her, Rand *would* be getting his book finished.

The weather was still pretty mild for early November, with only a slight chill in the air. For a while, anyway, Susan dismissed her worries about Rand and focused on his delightful niece and nephew. She couldn't wait till Penny was old enough to run and play.

Bonnie sat on a patio chair lavishing attention on Penny while Susan helped the kids set up an abbreviated version of a croquet court.

"You've done this before, Shane," Susan observed as the five-year-old whacked a red ball with his mallet and managed to get it through one of the wickets.

"I'm an expert," he declared.

"My turn! My turn!" Emily, the three-year-old, shrieked.

Susan barely dodged Emily's wildly swinging mallet, which missed the ball completely. "Can I help you, Emily?" Susan asked.

Emily nodded.

"Hey, no fair," Shane objected.

"Shane, remember what we talked about?" Bonnie

called from the patio. "Emily's a lot younger than you. It's not cheating if a grown-up helps her play."

Even with Susan's dubious help, Emily didn't win. Shane got his ball through the course in record time. When his ball hit the final stick, he crowed and did a victory dance worthy of any pro running back in the end zone.

"I'm the champ, I'm the champ! Hey, Uncle Rand, I won!" He raced toward the patio where Rand had appeared, standing in the French doors that led to his office. Unfortunately, in his haste the child tripped on a flagstone and fell knees first onto the edge of the patio.

He shrieked with pain and outrage. Bonnie gasped and came halfway out of her chair, but Rand was beside Shane in an instant, gently helping him to sit up, inspecting the boy's scraped knees. They were raw and oozing, but there wasn't a great amount of blood, thank God.

"Oh, man, you really did a number on those knees," he said, rubbing the child's back.

Shane sobbed against Rand's chest while Emily looked on solemnly. Susan took charge of Penny so Bonnie could comfort Shane if she wanted, but she hung back, letting Rand handle the crisis.

"It's okay to cry when something really, really hurts," Rand continued in a soothing voice.

Shane quieted after a minute or so.

"There, that's better. Think you can stand up?"

Shane nodded.

"I've got something inside we can put on those knees to make them feel better."

"Does it sting?"

"No, of course it doesn't sting. Would your favorite uncle put something on your knees that stings?"

Shane actually smiled. "I don't know. You might." He clung to Rand's hand as they went inside.

Susan and Bonnie hung back a little. "He's really good with kids," Bonnie said, "despite that cranky-uncle act he does."

"Yes, I can see that." She'd never expected to see Rand so soft, so tender. Of course, he'd been tender with her when she was having her baby, so she shouldn't have been so surprised.

"He really ought to have kids of his own," Bonnie said wistfully. "I think he'd like to. Unfortunately, that would require a wife. And the chances of Rand finding someone to marry are pretty marginal."

"Why would you say that?" Susan was more than a little surprised at Bonnie's assessment. Rand was exceptionally handsome. He was a doctor, a respected researcher. Maybe his social skills were a little on the thin side, but lots of really great men were introverts.

"He has the most disastrous track record with women you ever could imagine. You can't even guess how many nice girls I've shoved his way. It usually takes him about a week to send them screaming into the night."

"You're kidding."

"I'm not. He either bores them into a coma with his talk about skin eruptions, or he rushes them to bed, then goes to great pains to let them know it didn't mean anything to him. He's emotionally... retarded."

"He is not!" Susan couldn't believe how quickly and emphatically she came to Rand's rescue, but he did not strike her as emotionally retarded. "Sounds to me like he's afraid of risking his heart. And why shouldn't he be? It's a really cruel world out there."

"He's afraid to risk two Saturday nights in a row. No, I'm afraid he's doomed to a life of cantankerous bachelorhood." She gave Susan a sideways look. "Unless a very special woman can put up with him long enough to dig in and find the good parts."

"You're not looking at me, are you?" Susan asked, feeling a tinge of alarm. That was all Rand needed, a matchmaking sister trying to throw her at him.

"Nooooo, of course not." Bonnie shook her head so emphatically her dark hair whipped around her head. "You've got a lot on your plate right now. The last thing you need is an involvement with someone like Rand. Mmm, something smells good. I bet Rand was coming out to tell us dinner is ready."

Dinner proceeded more smoothly than Susan thought possible, given the turbulent few minutes preceding it. She learned that Bonnie's husband, Patrick, was an airline pilot, frequently out of town for days at a time.

"I'm home alone with the kids more than I care to be," she admitted. "But oh, those free tickets. We get to take the *best* vacations."

"Really? Where have you gone?" Susan had never

ventured farther than Florida, and that had been years ago on a family vacation to Disney World.

"Oh, you know, all the good places. London, Paris, Venice. I'm getting to be a real jet-setter, which is kind of a hoot, considering that before I met Patrick I'd never been in an airplane."

"Were you afraid of flying?" Susan asked, figuring the Barclay family must have done its share of traveling when the kids were growing up.

"Not afraid, just never had the opportunity. Mom wasn't big on vacations. Except for that one at the national park."

Rand frowned. "Don't remind me."

"You haven't met our mother, have you, Susan?" Bonnie asked.

"Grandmother Marjorie," Shane explained. "She don't like kids too much."

"*Doesn't* like," Bonnie automatically corrected, though she didn't deny the truth of Shane's assessment of his grandmother.

"Susan hasn't met Mom," Rand said. "And she probably won't."

"Why would your mother even want to meet me?" Susan asked with an offhand shrug. "I'm the hired help."

"That hasn't saved me," Clark said.

Bonnie laughed. "Are you kidding? Mom likes you better than me."

"I'd hate to see how she treats someone she *doesn't* like."

Susan wondered what in the world could be so bad

about Rand's mother. Then she decided Rand and Bonnie and Clark must be enjoying a private joke. Maybe Mrs. Barclay was a bit eccentric. Wealthy people often were.

"Isn't traveling with the children difficult?" Susan asked Bonnie to fill the silence.

"It can be a challenge. But sometimes just the two of us go."

"She dumps the kids on me," Rand said. He hadn't said much during the meal, but when he did venture forth with a comment, it was usually a grumpy one. Whether he was good with kids or not, maybe he really didn't like them.

The more time Susan spent with Rand's family, the more she realized how much they depended on Rand—maybe too much. There was a reason they all thought he was Saint Rand. He'd put off having his own life—including finding a wife and having children—to manage theirs.

Now he was managing hers. The sooner she got out of his life, the better—for both of them.

Chapter Nine

Rand managed to eke out three more pages that night, but he wasn't very happy with them. He was really distracted. Bonnie, Susan and the kids were watching videos in the TV room. The kids' shrill laughter sneaked under his door. He heard the baby crying, too, though that didn't last long—probably just long enough for a diaper change. And every so often, he thought he heard the musical notes of Susan's laughter, too.

It wasn't that the noise disturbed him. It was more a case of his wanting to join the fun.

Now, that was a new one on him. Normally he didn't care to be in any room where the women outnumbered the men, especially if he was the *only* man. Even among his own sisters he often felt awkward, inept and unnecessary. He'd served an important function for the family over the past few years—keeping food on the table and a roof over their heads. The rest he left to the womenfolk.

Then why suddenly did he want to be a part of the family fun?

Hell, he knew the answer. Susan. Ever since she'd come into his life, she'd disturbed his brain chemistry to the point he didn't feel like himself anymore.

After a fruitless search of his hard drive for an article he'd written two years ago, Rand called it quits. He shut down the computer, then wandered into the TV room. The domestic scene that greeted him gave him an odd pull.

It was nothing he hadn't seen before—kids and women. Shane and Emily were on the floor in front of the TV, engrossed in some cartoon. Penny was asleep on a blanket on his recliner, which was tipped back slightly so she couldn't roll out. And Bonnie and Susan sat together on the couch, where Bonnie was apparently teaching Susan how to knit.

"What in the name of heaven is that supposed to be?" Bonnie asked, examining the product emerging from Susan's needles. "You've got your knits and pearls all mixed up."

"Well, I can't tell the difference," Susan groused. "I'm knitting-dyslexic." This sent both women into peals of laughter. Rand wasn't sure he got the joke, or if he did, it wasn't that funny, but he enjoyed hearing them laugh.

Then Susan looked up and saw him, sobering immediately. "Uh-oh. Have we been too noisy? It's your sister's fault. She made me laugh so hard my tea almost came out my nose."

"Really?" Shane piped in.

"I only told her that if any man had to depend on

her knitting skills for a muffler, he would freeze to death.''

Rand perched on the sofa arm. ''Good thing there are other ways to keep men warm.'' Seeing the look on Bonnie's face, Rand wanted to slap his hand over his mouth. He hadn't really meant to say that aloud. His sister stared at him, her eyes wide, her mouth quirking as if she wanted to laugh.

Susan kept her gaze squarely on her handiwork. As she concentrated, the tip of her tongue peeked out from between her tightly pursed lips. It should have been cute, like when Alicia stuck out her tongue as she was learning to write. Instead, it was sexy.

Gary probably hadn't minded buying a muffler from the store, Rand thought uncharitably, just to remind himself exactly whose tongue he was admiring. A tongue that belonged to some other man, along with the moist pink lips and the tumble of dark hair and a body that was slimming down far too quickly for Rand's peace of mind.

''Well, you weren't too loud,'' Rand said. He'd thought he was coming in here to tell them all good night, that he was tired and going to bed. But the cozy scene drew him in. There was a place on the sofa calling his name, right next to Susan.

''The cartoon is almost over,'' Bonnie said. ''Then we get to watch something for grown-ups.''

Rand groaned. ''Not *Steel Magnolias* again, I hope.'' His sisters had watched that movie at least two dozen times.

''No. This time I brought *Pretty Woman.*''

"Even worse. Why can't we ever watch a good war movie? I think I have *Patton* around here somewhere."

Bonnie made a face. "Just sit down. If you don't like the movie, at least you can admire Julia Roberts's legs."

As if it were a huge imposition, Rand slid off the sofa arm and plopped down next to Susan. Who cared about Julia Roberts? He would rather watch Susan's strong, no-nonsense hands struggle with the delicate, feminine task of knitting, for which they were so obviously ill-suited.

"Did you get much writing done on your book?" Susan asked.

"Oh, Lord, don't get him started," Bonnie said as she switched out the videos amid her children's protests.

"I happen to think Rand's research is interesting," Susan objected. "I've never known a scientist before."

Oddly, Rand had no desire to wax enthusiastic about the efficacy of aloe vera on poison ivy, which he'd been engrossed in a few minutes ago. He felt this peculiar urge to talk about babies or knitting or, Lord help him, *Pretty Woman.* He remembered reading somewhere that if a man wanted to make a good impression on a woman, he should talk about subjects that interested her.

"I got a few pages done," he said. "What's that you're knitting?"

Susan looked at the lumpy, formless glob of pink

yarn dangling from her knitting needles. "I wanted to make Penny some booties," she said wistfully, "but by the time I get all my mistakes picked out, Penny will be going off to college."

He laughed, earning another look from Bonnie. Did he laugh that rarely?

Rand wondered if the movie was appropriate for the kids, but he needn't have worried. They were in dreamland before the opening credits finished. He'd always admired the way little kids could just drop off anywhere.

He sat there and watched the movie, and it wasn't as bad as he was afraid it would be.

Bonnie kept throwing suspicious glances his way.

When the movie ended, it was almost eleven. Susan said sleepy good-nights and took Penny upstairs. Rand helped his sister get her sleeping children buckled into the back seat.

"Thanks for letting us hang out here," she said. "Some nights, when Patrick's gone, I just can't face an evening without some adult conversation."

"It's not an imposition."

"Are you really working on your book? When I heard you'd invited a perfect stranger and her baby to live with you, I thought for sure it was just another excuse to procrastinate."

"I haven't been procrastinating. I've been setting the stage for—"

"Yeah, yeah, yeah." Bonnie waved away the rest of his explanation.

"Well, Susan is not my convenient excuse not to

write. I just couldn't turn her out onto the street. She had nowhere else to go."

Bonnie gave him a knowing look. "You've been saying you wanted some peace and quiet. But maybe that's not what you really wanted at all."

"Meaning?"

"Meaning, dear brother, that all these years I thought you were hopeless when it came to women. But I see now, it's just that you never really tried before. Tonight you were almost...charming."

"You think I was trying to impress Susan?" He did his best to make it sound like he thought her suggestion ridiculous. "I have no interest in Susan Kilgore or her ready-made family. She's in love with someone else, anyway."

Bonnie just crossed her arms and waited for him to hang himself. Which he did.

"Oh, hell. Am I that obvious?"

"To me. I don't think Susan sees it, though. So how does it feel to have your first crush?"

"Bonnie, come on. Yes, I find her attractive, but it's a moot point. She's in love with Penny's father."

"Then where is he?"

"No one's really sure. But I'm thinking of hiring someone to find him and drag his sorry ass back here."

"Rand, why?" Bonnie asked, sounding utterly bewildered.

"Because it's what Susan wants."

"And you want her to be happy. Oh, Rand, you've got it pretty bad."

He opened the driver's door of her car and nudged her inside. "Bonnie, go home. Forget we had this conversation. And don't you dare say anything to Mom or Betty or Alicia."

"Are you kidding? Alicia's the one who told me you had a case for your carpenter. And I don't even want to tell you what Mom has to say on the subject." She closed the door and started the engine.

SUSAN CAME INTO THE kitchen a week later as Clark pulled a pan of heavenly smelling muffins from the oven. "Mmm, please tell me those are for breakfast and not some cooking-school project."

"I made them just for you." He got out two plates and popped a couple of the muffins onto each.

"Just one for me, please," Susan said. "I'll have to get on the scales at my checkup today, and I want the news to be as encouraging as possible."

Clark froze just as he was about to set the plate down in front of her on the breakfast bar. "Your appointment's today?"

"Yes, at eleven. Oh, Clark, you're not going to cancel on me, are you?"

"No, no, of course not." He set down the plate distractedly and went to the calendar hanging on the back of the pantry door, then frowned.

"Come on, Clark, what is it?"

"I scheduled a makeup test for this morning," he admitted. "I forgot all about your appointment. But that's okay, I can re—"

"No, you can't miss that test again. I've still got

plenty of time to make other arrangements. In fact, maybe I'll just drive myself. It's been almost a month, and Arnette will probably give me the okay to drive, anyway."

"Rand would tar and feather me if I let you drive yourself. And who's going to take care of Penny while you're seeing the nurse?"

"I'll manage. Please don't worry so much about me, it'll be fine." She took a bite of muffin. "Mmm, these are heavenly. Are they at least a little bit healthy? Surely they contain a little whole-wheat flour? Or maybe wheat germ?"

"They're pure fat and sugar."

"I'm going to send Richard Simmons after you."

"I'm so afraid. Listen, why don't you call Bonnie or Alicia."

"You are worse than a Brownie den mother. I'm taking myself to the appointment, and that's final."

In truth, Susan was more than ready to assert her independence. Arnette *better* give her the okay to drive, and to get back to work, too. She had projects for Rand's house lined up and ready, and she needed to start earning her keep around here. She was tired of being a leech.

Besides, her muscles were getting soft. Her nails had actually started growing, and the other day Alicia had painted them for her. If she wasn't careful, she was going to take this stay-at-home mom thing too far.

Since Susan was left alone in the house, she decided to put some time in on the bookshelves. Mostly she did sanding and staining, work that was tedious and tiring, but not too physically challenging. Even overprotective Rand couldn't object.

She was amazed, though, how tired she was after only a couple of hours. She'd had visions of diving right into her work as soon as Arnette gave her the okay, immediately resuming her former level of activity. She realized she was going to have to work up to that.

She took a quick shower, dressed in jeans and a sweatshirt, changed Penny, then took the car seat and headed for the garage door. She remembered what Rand had said about not putting a baby in the front seat. Maybe while she was out she would go truck shopping.

She'd barely made it outside when a strange red truck pulled into the driveway. She paused to see who it was and was surprised to see Rand climb out of the driver's seat, leaving the engine running.

Oh, no, not again.

She figured he'd be ticked when he saw what she was about to do, but instead he smiled. "Your limo is here, Ms. Kilgore."

"Don't tell me Clark tattled on me."

"He did, as well he should have. You're not supposed to be driving."

"I will get the okay from Arnette today," she argued.

"You hope. And what about that truck?"

"I was planning on truck-shopping after my appointment. Speaking of trucks, what's with those wheels?'' She nodded toward the shiny red pickup.

''It's for you.''

''What?''

''It's got a small back seat. You can drive this truck until you're able to buy a new one for yourself. After Arnette gives you the okay, that is.''

Susan's head spun. ''But where did it—oh, never mind. Rand, you can't just go around making decisions like this for other people!''

He cocked his head and looked at her, as if he simply didn't understand what she was saying.

All right, she'd have to be more clear. ''Maybe this is what you're accustomed to with your sisters, but I'm not one of them. I've been forced to accept your charity up to this point—that or live in a homeless shelter. But that doesn't give you the right to make all of my decisions. So just take that truck back to wherever it came from.''

''You don't like it?'' he asked, looking more puzzled than offended. ''I could get a green one.''

In truth, she loved the truck. She loved the ruby-red color. She could see it with her business logo on the door. ''The color isn't the point. The point is…the point is…'' Oh, God, she'd forgotten the point. She couldn't think when he was looking at her that way.

''The point is,'' he said calmly, ''that you feel I'm treating you like a child.''

''No. You're treating me like I'm your responsibility. Which I most definitely am not. We have a business arrangement. I live in your house, I build stuff for you. Nothing more.''

That finally did it. He got mad. ''You have got more damn pride—look, damn it, I came home early so I could take you to your appointment and look after Penny. I borrowed the truck from a car-dealer friend of mine. It's used, and if you like it he'll cut you a deal. I thought I was being nice. I thought we were friends. I guess I was wrong.''

Susan didn't trust herself to speak. So few people had done nice things for her in her life, she didn't know how to act. She knew one thing, though; he'd just won this argument. How could she argue against a man who was so obviously trying to do something *good?*

He wasn't manipulating. He wasn't looking for gratitude or trying to play God. He was being nice. Without another word she handed Rand the car seat, then turned to fetch Penny.

They rode in semisilence for a few minutes. Susan spoke only to give Rand directions to Arnette's office, which the midwife shared with a supervising physician. When Susan had mulled over what she wanted to say, she finally spoke.

''Friendship is supposed to be a two-way street. And friends are supposed to respect each other's feelings and opinions. You're giving and giving, and I'm taking and taking, and you're determined to get your way no matter my opinion. You don't trust me to know what's good and right and safe for myself. And that doesn't feel like friendship. It feels like…like I'm being controlled. That's why I'm not acting as grate ful for your kindness as perhaps I should.''

He glanced over, then back to the road ahead. "Point taken. From now on I'll butt out.''

Shoot, this wasn't what she wanted. She obviously hadn't made him understand her point of view, but she didn't know what else to say.

SUSAN WAS CALLED IN FOR her exam almost as soon as she signed in, leaving Rand with Penny. The baby started crying the moment Susan was out of the room.

There were three other ladies in the waiting room, two with infants of their own—quiet, well-behaved children who weren't making a peep. All three women looked at Penny, then at Rand—accusingly, he thought.

He picked up Penny from her carrier and cuddled her. "C'mon, now, Penelope, let's not make such a fuss.''

The crying only increased. One of the other young mothers looked like she wanted to leap out of her seat and grab Penny from his incompetent hands. "It's amazing how quickly they become attached to their mothers,'' she said.

"Not mine,'' mother number two said, giving a pompous sniff. "She's a daddy's girl. My husband spends almost as much time taking care of Tiffany as I do, so she's used to him holding her. She's used to his voice.'' The woman looked at Rand. Her implication was clear, at least to him: *You obviously don't spend enough time with your baby if she's crying like that.*

He started to tell the ladies that he wasn't Penny's father, that he was just a friend doing a favor. But the words didn't come out of his mouth. Instead, he felt this silly urge to prove to them he was every bit as good at soothing a cranky baby as they were, in all their feminine wisdom.

That he was father material.

"Maybe she needs a change," the third woman suggested—and she didn't even have a baby, at least not with her.

Penny didn't need a change. Susan had just put a fresh diaper on her in the women's rest room not five minutes ago.

"It's not my face she doesn't like," he said. "It's not her diaper, and she's not hungry. She likes to move." With that he got up and started pacing.

Almost immediately, Penny quieted. He should have remembered how, that one night he'd baby-sat, she'd stopped crying only when he put her in the papoose and paced around the house until she'd fallen asleep.

"That's a good girl," he crooned, giving mother number one a smug look. And then Penny spit up on his shirt.

All three women jumped up to help. One mopped him up with her own baby's spit-up cloth, which she'd had draped over her shoulder. Another one rushed to get some water. The third fluttered ineffectually, saying, "Oh, dear, oh, dear."

Rand's concern was for Penny. He knew babies regurgitated all the time, but he couldn't recall ever seeing Penny do it. He took the baby back, studying her face, feeling her forehead, then went to the receptionist. "Could I borrow a baby thermometer?"

The receptionist found a thermometer that could be lain across the baby's forehead. While Rand waited a few moments for Penny's temperature to register, he prayed he wouldn't have to tell Susan that Penny was sick. Thus far Penny had been extraordinarily healthy.

Fortunately, her temperature was completely normal. She looked bright-eyed and had good color. Recalling his long-ago pediatrics rotations, he gently palpitated her abdomen, but she didn't look the least bit uncomfortable. He checked her eyes with a penlight, and the pupils contracted normally. Her ears looked good. In fact, she seemed a lot more cheerful now that she'd gotten rid of that sour milk in her tummy.

Rand returned the thermometer. "Nervous father," mother number one murmured to the others, plenty loud enough for him to hear.

"Shoot, you should see my husband when Tiffany spits up," mother number two said. "He runs the other direction so fast he could win the Olympics. It wouldn't occur to him to take her temperature. A dirty diaper's even worse."

So much for the daddy's girl, Rand thought.

"Mine, too," mother number three said. And they all beamed at Rand. The room's atmosphere had changed dramatically.

Rand decided to take Penny for a walk.

"THEN I CAN DRIVE?" Susan said when Arnette completed her exam, pronouncing her patient in good shape. "Please tell me I can drive."

"Yes, you can drive. Though I don't feel too comfortable about that old truck of yours. You should have Penny in a back seat."

"So I've heard. Don't worry, I've got a new truck." She wasn't sure when she'd decided to take up Rand's offer. But she was dealing with Penny's safety, here, and it was stupid of her to turn down Rand's perfectly sensible loan of a safer truck because of her pride. She would talk to his dealer friend and find out what kind of terms he would negotiate, if he would give her anything for her old truck as a trade in.

"How about my work? Can I go back to my carpentry?"

"I don't see why not."

"No restrictions?" she asked, just to be sure.

"Nothing beyond ordinary precaution when lifting and moving anything heavy. People in your profession suffer a lot of injuries, and usually because they weren't careful."

"I'll be careful," Susan promised.

Arnette flashed a sly smile. "You didn't ask me about sex."

"My mother told me about the birds and the bees," Susan said primly.

"You know what I mean. That's usually the first question my patients ask after childbirth. When can I make love again?"

"Now why would I need to know that?" Susan asked dryly.

"How about that gorgeous hunk you're living with?"

"Arnette! It's not like that, and you know it."

Arnette was studying her. "I know your eyes go all soft at the mention of him."

"Baloney," Susan mumbled.

"So how are things in the big house?"

"If you really want to know…weird. Rand and his whole family have adopted me like a stray dog with puppies."

"Well, somebody needed to."

Susan paused in tying her tennis shoe. "I'm that bad, huh?"

"You *were* that bad. You're much better, now. But when you first started coming to me, you were like a broken doll. I worried a lot about what would become of you."

"You think I'm better now? I'm a charity case."

Arnette sighed with exasperation. "Think of it as someone giving you a break. That's all too rare in our society. Enjoy it. Take advantage of the fact you've been given some breathing space. Figure out where you need to be and how to get there. And don't be in such a hurry to leap. A girl could do worse than Rand Barclay."

Susan laughed, pulling the laces of her shoe so tight it pinched. "I have no designs on Rand Barclay."

"You sure?"

Susan wasn't sure at all. "Well, let's put it this way. He doesn't have any designs on me. He's married to his work. And rich doctors don't hook up with single-mother-carpenters. He could have any woman he wanted." If he put his mind to it.

"Maybe he wants you."

"He's already said he just wants to be friends."

"That works. Love at first sight is a myth, anyway. Real love has to start somewhere smaller—with kindness, admiration, friendship."

"How about lust?" Susan quipped.

"That works, too."

Susan laughed again, though the word *friendship* vibrated in her head. That's what Rand thought they were—friends. Could it possibly lead somewhere else?

"Um, just for the record," Arnette said, "it's fine for you to have intercourse."

"I won't be."

"Just in case, I'll give you these." She handed Susan a sample pack of birth control pills. "Not to be too pushy, but Penny was unplanned. It's best to be prepared."

"They're okay to take while I'm nursing?"

"This kind is safe."

Susan decided it was easier to accept the pills than to argue that she wouldn't need them, not now, at any rate. She gave Arnette a goodbye hug, wrote out a check from her ever-dwindling bank account, handed it through the window to the receptionist, then headed into the waiting room. Rand and Penny were nowhere.

She felt a silly, momentary panic, until one of the women waiting there pointed toward the door. "He took her for a walk. That's one awesome husband you got there. You don't see many men that dedicated to caring for their baby."

"Oh, he's not..." Susan stopped. She would probably never see any of these women again. "Yes, he's wonderful, isn't he? Penny just adores him."

She grabbed Penny's carrier and diaper bag and exited the office, feeling really silly. But it sure had felt good to pretend, once again, that Rand was Penny's father.

She caught a glimpse of Rand and Penny at the end of the hall where it opened out into the lobby. He was pacing the marble floor with Penny cradled against his chest, looking quite at home. Anyone who saw him would assume he was Penny's father.

As she came closer, she thought Rand was talking to her. Then she realized he was singing.

The gruff bear of a man was singing a lullaby to her baby, in the softest, sweetest, gentlest baritone she'd ever heard.

She thought she heard a *ping* coming from inside her chest, then realized it wasn't so much something she'd heard as something she'd felt.

Just like that, she'd fallen in love.

Chapter Ten

Rand heard the thud-thud of Susan's tennis shoes coming down the hall, and he abruptly stopped singing. It wouldn't do to have anyone find out he'd gone soft. But Penny was just so cute, he couldn't help himself. He'd felt tender feelings for his nieces and nephews when he'd held them, when they'd smiled at him despite the fact he never tried to make them smile, when they'd grabbed onto his finger with impossibly tiny hands.

But he'd never felt like this about a baby before. Penny just seemed so helpless. To begin with, she was the tiniest baby he'd ever held. She'd grown some, but even at a month old she still looked like a newborn. Then there was the fact that she had no father of her own.

Susan appeared in the lobby, a strange expression on her face. "What are you doing all the way out here?"

"Penny wanted to move," he said. "You know how she is." He didn't want to tell Susan that he'd started feeling like a chicken among three coyotes in that waiting room.

Those women had made him feel decidedly uncomfortable—as women usually did, even though all they'd done was help him deal with Penny's momentary lack of composure and compliment his fathering abilities. He supposed he hadn't wanted Susan to appear and realize he'd been posing as her husband.

"How was your checkup?"

"Fine." She broke into a big smile. "Arnette says I can drive and I can get back to work. No restrictions."

Rand flashed her a suspicious look as he passed the sleeping baby to her. "*No* restrictions?"

"None." She smiled up at him, and for the first time he could remember, she looked truly happy. Radiant, even. He was almost irresistibly drawn to the warmth and light she radiated, and he had to force himself to step back, to turn, to head for the parking lot.

"I still wish you'd take it easy," he said, holding the door open for her as she fastened Penny into her car seat. "Childbirth is an enormous physical trauma—"

"You're telling me?"

"—and it takes a while to heal."

"I'm going to start calling you Mother Hen."

Rand winced and said nothing more as she opened the truck door and settled Penny into the back seat. That wasn't how he wanted Susan to think of him.

Exactly how do *you want Susan to think of you?* his inner voice asked.

"Like someone who cares," he said aloud as they both climbed into the pickup.

"What?"

"Can't you just let me care about you without fighting it tooth and nail? Has no one ever worried about you?"

"Not in a long time," she admitted. "You're right, I'm not used to it."

"Then let me do it. Let me say the words. Just because I want you to be careful doesn't mean I think you don't have good judgment or intelligence or whatever. It just means...I would feel terrible if anything happened to you. Or Penny."

He looked at her, willing her to meet his gaze, to see something of what he felt. Maybe she could make sense of it, because he sure couldn't.

The atmosphere in the truck became supercharged. He was acutely aware of the heightened color in her cheeks, the scent of her, the uncooperative strand of hair that wouldn't stay tucked behind her ear. He reached to smooth the hair off her face and ended up drawing her to him. Although maybe she leaned in of her own accord. He was never sure. The only thing he could be sure about later was that it was the most explosive, mind-blowing kiss he'd ever shared with a woman.

And this time, she was kissing him, Rand Barclay, not some fantasy man from her dreams. Her arms slid around his neck and she angled her head, deepening the kiss, almost devouring him with her sudden hunger.

He wanted her with a fierceness that took him by surprise. He cursed the fact they were in the front seat of a truck in a very public parking lot—with a baby in the back seat.

Apparently Susan hadn't forgotten their awkward location, either. She eased away from the kiss, turning wanton passion into a warm if slightly desperate hug.

"Rand," she whispered, clinging to him tightly, "what are we doing?"

He longed to make light of it, to diffuse the situation, to write it off as an unwise impulse. But to do so would be insulting to Susan. He was the one who'd set the serious mood with his talk of caring. It wouldn't be fair to mitigate the significance of what had just happened. The attraction between them wasn't going away.

"We were kissing," he said in all seriousness, as if she hadn't figured that out.

"We can't."

"Apparently we can."

"I mean, I don't know what you have in mind, a fling or a casual affair or if you want me to be your girlfriend or what," she said all in a rush, "but I'm just not ready. I mean, physically I'm okay. Arnette said—" She stopped herself and pulled away, embarrassed.

"Arnette said what?"

"Never mind. But my life is in such a turmoil right

now. I'm getting my business back off the ground and learning to be a mother, and there's Gary, too.''

''Ah, Gary.'' He suspected that was the real problem. ''I guess it always comes back to him.''

''I can't argue with biology. He's Penny's father, and he'll always be her father.''

For some reason, that comment hurt.

''I'll find him eventually,'' she said. ''He'll have to come back here to at least meet his daughter. And when he does—''

''You don't want him to find you shacked up with a new boyfriend.''

''I just don't want things to be too complicated. I want to give Gary the chance to be a real father, and I want Penny to have a chance at a real family.''

''You mean you want to marry him.''

She hesitated a long time before answering. ''If that's what he wants…yes, I'll marry him. We had a good thing for a while. Well, it wasn't that good. I was pretty mixed up. But we had potential.''

''I see.''

''No, I don't think you do. If you and I had met at some other time…oh, God, that's really a cliché, isn't it.''

''Yeah.'' He was trying real hard not to be angry with her for rejecting him. He'd been ready to take her home, carry her upstairs, and ravish her like a woman ought to be ravished. It wasn't her fault she felt she owed some loyalty to the jerk who'd abandoned her. ''All right, I'll try really hard not to kiss you again. But I expect some effort on your part. That kiss was half your doing.''

"I know, I know. I wasn't trying to blame you for anything.''

He tried to catch her eye, to smile and let her know he was okay with her decision. But she wasn't looking at him, she was staring at his shirt.

"Why is your shirt all wet?''

"Oh, that. Penny spit up.''

Susan looked stricken, and the kiss was quickly pushed aside. "She did?'' She craned her neck to look at the baby, who was gurgling happily. "She never does that.''

"She's fine. I took her temperature, did a quickie exam. She probably was just car sick.''

"Are you sure?'' Susan felt the sleeping baby's forehead.

"You'll want to keep an eye on her, but she seems healthy to me. Babies spit up all the time.''

Rand started the truck, grateful for something to keep his hands occupied, something to keep his attention firmly focused on. His whole body still thrummed from the after-effects of that kiss, and it would have taken very little prompting for him to reach for the alluring Susan again.

He ought to be grateful she was being so sensible. The very last thing he needed in his life right now was a woman. He had a book to finish, deadlines, research to verify, interviews to conduct, numbers to crunch and re-crunch. In addition, he was in charge of a Phase II clinical study being conducted with a new topical ointment next month. He did not have time to go gaga over Susan.

And even if he did, she could do so much better. Not that he was in the habit of demeaning himself. He thought rather a lot of himself, actually. He was smart, sensible, practical and responsible. He imagined that he would be faithful and reasonably unselfish.

But not now! Not when he'd been waiting all these years for his solitude, his quiet house, his long evenings with his books in front of the fire. Susan deserved a fatherly type who was ready to marry her and become Penny's dad. Not Gary, but someone else.

And speaking of Gary, damn it, why didn't his private investigator friend have more news? A guy like Gary couldn't be that hard to find. The sooner Gary came back into Susan's life, the sooner she would see he was a loser, send him packing, and get over him.

So she can move on to you?

WHEN SUSAN WAS FINALLY alone in her bedroom, she replayed the memory of Rand's kiss about a dozen times, embellishing the details, wondering how much of it really happened and how much was fantasy. She was appalled at how readily she'd fallen into his arms—yet she wouldn't erase the kiss for anything.

The fact that Rand cared about her in any fashion made her heart glow. She recognized the fact that he didn't feel the same as she did. He felt responsible toward her, he perhaps desired her, he might even pity her, but he certainly didn't love her.

She didn't imagine that would change. Rich, accomplished research scientists fell in love with homeless waifs only in Cinderella fairy tales. She would have to move on with her life. But she could live on the memory of that kiss for quite some time.

A tapping on her door broke her out of her reverie. "Come in," she called.

The door crept open and Alicia poked her head in. "Hope I'm not bothering you. Rand said you had a busy day today."

Busier than it ought to have been. "You could never bother me. Come in."

Alicia slipped inside. "I hate to spring this on you unannounced, but Mom and I were shopping for honeymoon clothes, and she decided to drop in on Rand. Rand asked us to stay for supper."

"That's wonderful. I'd like to meet your mother." And satisfy her own curiosity.

Alicia looked uneasy. "Yeah, she's been dying to meet you, too."

"What do you mean? How does she even know I exist?"

"Oh, well, I might have mentioned you in passing and, well, let's just say…Mom's not always the most pleasant, open-minded, flexible—"

"Oh, Lord, she thinks I'm an opportunist shacking up with her baby boy."

"Something like that. She's also an incredible snob."

Now certain things were making sense—the way Rand had virtually ignored her curiosity about his mother, the fact that he hadn't invited Marjorie over during the weeks Susan had been living here. Rand's sisters were so nice, Susan had just assumed his mother couldn't be too terrible.

"So am I to give a command performance?"

"Unless you want to plead a migraine—and that might be your best bet."

It was a tempting suggestion, but Susan had a feeling she couldn't avoid Marjorie Barclay forever. "Of course I'll meet your mother. I'm sure we'll get along fine, once she meets me and sees I have no designs on the family fortune."

"It's your funeral. Oh, Mom said to tell you the dress code's casual, and we're eating at eight."

"Okay." Susan didn't mention that she was starving, that she would pass out if she didn't get something to eat before eight. She would go down early and help Clark in the kitchen and nab a few raw carrots. Clark had unbent slightly about having her touch his pots and pans. He'd even been showing Susan how to prepare some of his recipes.

But first, her wardrobe. She wasn't taking any chances. Mrs. Barclay's version of "casual" might very well mean a cocktail-length dress rather than floor length. Alicia wore a skirt and blouse, so Susan took her faithful black skirt from the closet and paired it with an amber fake-cashmere sweater. She wasn't going to show up at the dinner table looking like some homeless orphan—even though that's what she was.

"Is that woman ever going to make an appearance?" Marjorie Barclay, Rand's mother, asked as she swirled her martini. "Or is she going to hide up in her room? What's she afraid of, anyway?"

"You have to ask?" Rand took a sip of his own martini, which his mother had insisted on mixing for him. He didn't even like martinis, and this one was strong enough to render an elephant unconscious. "Anyway, Susan is probably resting." *And she'd probably rather meet up with the Spanish Inquisition than get interrogated by my mother.*

The four of them—Rand, Marjorie, Alicia and Dougy—were in the living room, which he entered only when his mother was here. She had decorated it, and it looked more like a museum than a home—an eclectic museum. Fussy antiques from several different periods were crammed into the cavernous room, along with a contemporary leather sofa. The effect was unsettling and claustrophobic.

"Don't be cheeky. I have no intention of being unpleasant to the girl. I simply feel someone ought to be asking her some pointed questions about her plans. Otherwise, she'll be here indefinitely."

"Maybe Rand wants her here indefinitely," Alicia interjected.

Rand gave her a warning look. "Mother, I don't want you to ask her any questions. I'm the one who dragged her here and insisted she stay. She had some bad luck—"

"Getting pregnant without a husband is bad planning, not bad luck," Marjorie said with a sniff as she checked for dust on an end table.

"Something you and I know a little something about," Alicia groused.

"—and she's here for however long it takes her to find another situation," Rand continued, "and that's final. Haven't you ever heard the saying, 'Charity begins at home'?"

"That saying means you're supposed to be kind and generous with your family first. It doesn't mean you're supposed to bring strangers to live in your house and sponge off you."

Alicia cleared her throat rather loudly. Rand turned, and just as he feared, Susan stood in the doorway with Penny. How much had she heard? He'd been dreading this meeting for a long time. At least he'd shielded Susan from his mother when she was weakest and most vulnerable. She was stronger now, and he figured she had what it took to handle whatever Marjorie dished out.

Susan smiled warmly and didn't seem as if she'd heard anything upsetting. Good.

Rand hopped to his feet. "Susan, how nice you look. This is my mother, Marjorie Barclay. Mother, Susan Kilgore."

Susan came forward, her hand extended. "How nice to finally meet you. Please don't get up."

Marjorie didn't even start to stand up. "Pleasure," she said, giving Susan's hand a perfunctory squeeze.

"Mama, baby!" Dougy announced, toddling over to Susan and looking up at Penny.

"Hi, Dougy!" Susan said, stooping down so the little boy could see Penny better. "You remember Penny?"

Dougy reached for Penny, but Alicia was faster, swooping him out of reach. "Oh, no, Dougy. Look at the baby but don't grab." She turned to Marjorie. "Look, Mom, isn't she adorable?"

Marjorie peered down her nose at Penny. "Mmm, yes, cute. Who's going to look after the baby while we eat dinner?"

Susan's smile fled her face. "Oh. Well, I thought I would. She'll be good. She just woke up from a nap."

"Nonsense. Clark can watch the children."

Susan opened her mouth to object, but Rand shook his head almost imperceptibly, silencing whatever she was about to say.

"I'm sure Clark will be delighted to watch the children for a few minutes," Rand said. "If we can pry Penny out of Susan's arms."

Susan's smile returned at his teasing. "I'm not that bad. I let you take care of her this afternoon."

Marjorie frowned disapprovingly.

"Do you want something to drink?" Rand asked. "We have wine, or I can mix you something. Mom makes a good martini."

"Mmm, you know what I'd really like?" Susan asked.

Rand could only imagine.

"A beer. I haven't had a beer since before I was pregnant."

"I'm afraid we don't have any beer in the bar," Marjorie said imperiously.

"No problem. I think I saw some in the kitchen fridge. Be right back." Susan left the room with a bouncy step.

"Well," Marjorie said when Susan was out of ear-shot, "doesn't that just figure. Beer."

"Mom!" Alicia objected. "There's nothing wrong with beer."

Rand seemed to recall a case or two of Pabst Blue Ribbon in Marjorie's past, but if he mentioned it she would deny it to her death. Her memory was highly selective.

"Beer is fine when you're watching a football game, I suppose," Marjorie said, "but it doesn't make the best impression. Anyway, she should have taken something that was offered."

"Nonsense," Rand said. "I've told her to make herself at home here. If she wants something out of the kitchen, why shouldn't she have it?"

"And what are you doing baby-sitting her child, for Pete's sake? How is someone like her ever going to learn responsibility if people like you give her everything she wants and jump at her beck and call?"

Rand pinched the bridge of his nose. "Give it a rest, huh, Mom?"

Alicia gasped and Marjorie almost choked on her martini.

"You don't even know Susan," he continued. "And even if you did, you have no right to judge her. She's a good human being and a dedicated mother.

She is my guest in my home. And I warn you, if you say one unkind word to her, just one word that is anything but friendly and gracious, I will ask you to leave."

Marjorie straightened her spine. "Well, then, I guess I'll save you the trouble." She set her glass on the coffee table and rose a bit unsteadily.

"C'mon, Mom, you can't leave," Alicia said. "'Cause I'm driving."

"Then I'll call a taxi." She pulled a cell phone from her purse, pushed a speed-dial button, and headed for the door as she spoke to a dispatcher.

"Rand, you can't just let her leave," Alicia said.

"Why not?"

"Rand…"

"Oh, all right." He followed Marjorie out of the living room, catching her at the front door. He didn't feel he owed her an apology, but he would give her one anyway. But only because if his mother didn't show up at the dinner table, Susan would ask where she was. And no matter what he said, Susan would know she had somehow been at the root of Marjorie's sudden change of plans.

SUSAN ESCAPED TO THE kitchen, where Clark was putting the final touches on dinner. She didn't want a beer. She just wanted to escape the visceral tensions in the living room and regroup.

It was obvious Marjorie detested her on sight. The older woman saw Susan as a threat and would do what she could to drive Susan and Rand apart.

Not that Rand would let his mother manipulate him. He was stronger than that. But Susan wasn't quite that strong. The sudden realization that Rand's mother wasn't going to *ooh* and *aah* over Penny had almost driven Susan to tears. She could just imagine how she would react if Marjorie really sharpened her claws and launched a full frontal attack.

"You didn't last long in the lioness's den."

Susan grabbed a deviled egg from a plate with one hand while jiggling Penny with the other. "My God, she's a dragon."

Clark frowned at the plate she'd just tampered with. "Now look what you've done. You messed up the symmetry." He fussed over the plate, rearranging the remaining eggs. "Marjorie's not that bad once you get to know her. She's just really, really suspicious of strangers. Once you have her in your court, though, she'll defend you to the death."

"Is she in your court?"

"Oh, yeah, she likes me fine. She likes ordering me around, too, like she's Scarlett O'Hara, but that's okay. It's all part of the fantasy."

"What fantasy?" Susan dug an imported beer out of the fridge for show, but she didn't drink it.

"Oh, nothing," he murmured. "Is she really being a witch?"

"She was civil to my face. But just as I was walking into the room, she was talking about how I sponged off Rand. And she looked at Penny like she was a cockroach."

"Uh-oh, the ultimate sin. She didn't go ape over your kid."

"I guess I'm being silly. I'll try to get along with her."

"That's all you can do."

Susan put Penny in her swing, which was set up in the kitchen, then helped Clark carry dishes of steaming food into the dining room. She was more or less hired help, after all, and she supposed she ought to act like it. Maybe Mrs. Barclay would like her better if she thought Susan wasn't playing lady of the manor.

Dinner was tense but civil enough. Undercurrents passed between Rand and his mother, which Susan didn't understand. But Alicia kept giving Susan encouraging smiles and drawing her out in conversation, so it wasn't terrible. Marjorie announced she had to go just as soon as she took her last bite of pie, and no one tried to talk her into staying.

Susan said good-night, then reclaimed her baby and fled upstairs. It wasn't bad enough she'd fallen in love; she had to go and fall in love with someone who was completely out of her league.

"COME ON, SWEETIE, EAT A little of the nice formula."

Penny's pediatrician had recommended that Susan start very slowly to wean Penny from mother's milk. Susan would be going back to her carpentry very soon, and it wouldn't be practical to take the baby with her on various jobs. She would have to arrange for childcare of some sort—and Penny would have to get her meals from a bottle. If she had any trouble with formula, now was the time to find out.

But so far, Penny had flatly refused to have anything to do with the bottle Susan offered. The nurses at the hospital had apparently gotten her to drink from a bottle, though the bottle had contained real mother's milk.

So the problem might be the formula, not the nipple. Nothing Susan did could convince Penny to widen her culinary preferences.

"You are spoiled rotten, you know that?" Susan was about to untie her robe—she'd finally gotten herself a robe—and give Penny what she really wanted when someone tapped softly on the door.

"Come in."

Rand entered very slowly. His eyes were closed. "Susan? You're decent, right?"

"Yes, fully clothed."

He opened his eyes. "It's just that you were sitting there with Penny in the rocker, and I wasn't sure."

"We're trying a bottle tonight," Susan said, talking louder over Penny's increasingly verbal displeasure. "'Trying' is the operative word."

"Let me try."

"You?"

"Hey, why not? She likes me, and she certainly can't get any other kind of meal from me."

"Be my guest." She handed Rand the bottle and the squirming baby, then offered him the rocking chair, but he chose to pace instead. Miracle of miracles, after a bit of coaxing, she took the artificial nipple and started sucking.

"Well, I'll be darned," Susan said in wonder.

"Told ya so." He was silent a few moments, absently patting Penny's diapered bottom as he paced a few steps one way, then another. "I came here to apologize for tonight."

"I'm the one who should apologize. The last thing I wanted to do was cause dissension in your family."

"You didn't do anything. My mother's behavior was horrendous."

"I don't blame her for being suspicious. I am taking advantage, after all."

"I wish you wouldn't think of it that way."

"It's true. Your mother's right. I'm a sponge."

"Oh. So you heard that."

"Yeah."

"She'll warm up to you. And you're not a sponge."

"What else would you—Rand?" Panic welled up in Susan's throat like a tidal wave. "Penny's not breathing!"

Chapter Eleven

Rand dropped the bottle onto the carpet and peered at Penny. Her little mouth was overflowing with formula, and she looked distressed.

She's choking.

Rand's emergency medical training kicked in. He flipped Penny over, placed his fingers over her breastbone, then gave her back a firm, sharp push. Formula spilled onto the carpet and Penny coughed once, twice.

Susan hovered nearby, her face a sickly white, but to her credit she stayed out of his way. He'd seen mothers in emergency rooms try to grab small children out of doctor's hands when they didn't understand what the doctor was doing.

Rand thumped Penny on the back a couple more times, walking a careful line between applying the necessary firmness and breaking her fragile little bones. She coughed again, then started howling in outrage.

"It's all right," Rand said to Susan. "She's breathing."

Susan took the baby from his shaking hands and attempted to comfort her. "What happened?" she demanded. "Why did she stop breathing like that? Is she going to be all right?"

"She choked on the formula. It was my fault. I should have been watching her more closely."

"Oh, Rand, please, don't blame yourself. It could have just as easily been me holding her. You didn't hurt her, you saved her life. Thank God you knew what to do."

Rand certainly didn't feel much like a hero.

Penny quieted after a minute or two. She seemed none the worse for her ordeal.

"Is there something else we should do?" Susan asked, holding the baby as if she never wanted to let her go again. "Should we take her to the emergency room? Or...or..."

"If it would make you feel better, we can do that. But she seems fine now. It's not uncommon for a baby to get a little milk down the wrong way."

"But she's never done that before. Is it the bottle?"

"It might be. Babies have to suck differently on an artificial nipple than on the, um, real thing."

"Then I'll breast-feed her till she's twenty-one."

Rand smiled. "She'll get the hang of the bottle. Try it again in a couple of weeks."

"She's asleep."

"And breathing quite normally."

"Still, I'm going to put the bassinet right next to the bed tonight."

And she would probably wake up every ten minutes and check to see that Penny was breathing.

Still feeling partially responsible for Penny's close call, Rand followed Susan through the connecting bathroom and into her bedroom. He only wanted to see Penny safely tucked in for the night, he told himself. But he also wasn't quite ready to say good-night to Susan.

Susan settled Penny into her bassinet, then moved the tiny bed right next to her own bed, where the baby would be mere inches from where Susan would sleep. Then she sat down on the edge of the bed and stared at her child's sleeping form. She wrapped her arms around herself as if she was freezing cold.

She trembled so forcefully Rand could see it.

He sat down beside her, concerned. "Are you going to be all right?"

She nodded almost spasmodically. A tear glinted on one cheek. "I'm fine, really."

"No, you're not." He put his arms around her, determined to comfort her. "It's okay. It's over now."

"But what if it happens again?"

"It probably won't. You can call Dr. Bagley tomorrow, but I think she'll be just fine." He rubbed Susan's back and stroked her hair.

"I've never been so scared in my whole life."

"Mothers are scared all the time for their children. It's a survival mechanism. I've lived my life around mothers in various stages. I know what I'm talking about."

"You mean this doesn't get better? I'll spend the rest of my life terrified?"

"Not all the time. But you'll never stop worrying—at least, not completely."

"I guess your mother still worries about you."

"And she shows it in her own, unique way."

Susan relaxed a little and leaned against him. "I guess she sees me as some terrible threat to her little boy."

And Marjorie wasn't that far off the mark, Rand thought uneasily. Susan was one hell of a threat to his peace of mind, not to mention the life plan he'd mapped out for himself for the next few years—a plan that didn't involve women and children.

"She'll get over it."

"It's no wonder you're not married, though. Does she put all your girlfriends through this kind of wringer?"

"Are you kidding? I've never let her meet anyone I was dating. Anyway, it's never been necessary. A lot of things scare women away from me before my mother even gets to take a whack at them."

"You drive them away?"

"Not on purpose. It's more like they...drift. But that's okay with me. I've never really needed a woman hanging around. I've got my hands full with work."

"Work doesn't keep you warm at night."

"That's what electric blankets are for." And he was the biggest liar. He did get lonely sometimes, even when his family and Clark were everywhere he turned. But at least he'd distracted Susan to where she was no longer crying.

"Will you be okay now?" he asked gently.

She nodded. "I'll be fine."

"I could stay for a while."

"No."

Her sharp tone startled him. Okay, she wanted him gone. He wasn't one to overstay his welcome. He eased his arms from around her.

Suddenly she clung to him with a sweet desperation. "Oh, please don't go. I didn't mean it. Stay with us. Stay with *me*," she corrected herself. "Be with me. I need you."

His body responded to her words before his mind could—before he could form any words of protest, any sensible response. He simply pulled her closer and kissed her, long and hard, his sudden desperation a good match for hers.

He kissed her for what seemed like forever—her mouth, her jaw, her chin. Held her face between his hands and searched her eyes for some sign that she wanted him to stop, but the passion that glazed her eyes like mist on a midnight sky did nothing but encourage him.

He needed more—he wanted to be closer.

He fumbled with the sash of her robe. His hands felt like they had ten thumbs each, but eventually he got the bow at her waist undone and the robe fell open, revealing her thin cotton nightshirt. His breath caught in his throat at the sight of her milk-engorged breasts straining against the pale pink cotton.

He grasped her shoulders and kissed her again, throwing caution out the window this time. He kissed her passionately, hungrily, and in a manner that gave her no doubt as to where he was going. His blood roared in his ears, and he could feel her pulse everywhere he touched her. He slid the robe down her shoulders and caressed her bare arms. Her skin was still cool to the touch, but quickly warming.

They didn't talk. There didn't seem to be any need. They removed clothing in a heated rush, then fell together onto the bed in a tangle of writhing limbs and pleasured sighs.

He rolled over onto his back and pulled her on top of him, stroking her strong, slender back and the curve of her bottom, memorizing the satiny feel of her skin, so soft where the sun never touched it. He wanted to hold her like this forever—or as long as it took to chase that scared look out of her eyes for at least a few minutes.

SUSAN FELT LIKE HER BRAIN had short-circuited. Wasn't there something…something she should be doing? But Rand obviously needed no instructions. Wherever he touched her, she caught her breath. Wherever he kissed her, she wanted more. He pleasured her body with the thoroughness and precision she might expect from a doctor-scientist—one intimately familiar with anatomy. He left no corner of her body undiscovered. He found every ticklish spot, every place that made her squirm, every sensitive spot that made her quiver with passion.

"Are you sure?" he said in a strained whisper when she got brave enough to stroke his body. "Are you sure it's not too soon? I don't want to hurt you."

If he hadn't already won her over this afternoon with his lullaby, this question would have done the trick. She knew, without a doubt, that if she suddenly said she'd changed her mind, he would stop, no matter what discomfort it caused him. She had that much trust in him.

"I almost told you this afternoon. Arnette said it's okay to...to do this." So that he didn't mistake her intention, her wishes, she opened to him, inviting him settle in the cradle between her legs.

He spent a long time poised to enter her, moving with agonizing slowness, testing her. But she felt no discomfort at all, only a raging need to have him fill her up. When he finally entered her she was more than ready, yet he took his sweet time, letting her savor every new sensation. Though there was no pain, she was extraordinarily sensitive to the light friction he created.

She cried out when her desire peaked, remembering Penny was a few feet away only when the baby woke up and started crying.

"Oops," Susan whispered, slapping one hand over her mouth, though Penny's cries didn't bother her too much. If the baby was crying, she was breathing.

Rand laughed, then squeezed his eyes shut, and the laughter became a cry of exultation as he released inside her.

He held her a few more moments, then moved his

weight off of her. She put her head on his shoulder and listened to her baby as Penny quieted and went back to sleep. He stroked Susan's hair and said very little.

She loved the tenderness, almost more than the sex itself. Gary had always held her after they made love, because she expected it, but she always got the sense that he wanted to either roll over and go to sleep or get up and do something else.

She didn't get that feeling with Rand. He seemed peaceful, content to just quietly hold her.

"Are you warm enough?" he asked after a while.

"Yes."

"You want me to stay the night?"

"Definitely."

"Do you have an alarm clock?"

She laughed. "Yeah, a six-and-a-half-pound one."

"Oh, right."

"Trust me, you won't oversleep." She paused. "You don't have to stay if you don't want to." She wasn't going to repeat the mistakes she made with Gary. She might be in love with Rand, but she wasn't just going to crack open her heart and hand it to him. She was going to love him, but she wasn't going to need him.

"Now, let's see," he said. "Sleep with a beautiful, warm woman curled up next to me, or sleep in a cold, empty bed. Hmm, tough decision."

"You do have that electric blanket."

"I don't. I lied about that. Susan…"

She held her breath. He was going to tell her this

was a mistake, that this couldn't happen again, that they'd lost their minds...

"Look at you, you're all tensed up. You really expect the worst, don't you."

"I don't know."

"I was just going to say that I know this isn't what either of us planned, and I know it complicates things a bit, but we'll take things one day at a time, okay?"

She forced herself to relax. "Okay."

"But you have to be honest with me. I don't want to be Gary's surrogate."

"I could never get you and Gary mixed up. Make no mistake, Rand, tonight I wanted you and no one else. I've been doing my best to be strong and independent, but this one night I was at the end of my tether. I needed to be close to someone—to you, I mean."

He was quiet, unnervingly quiet.

"You think I'm too needy, right?"

"Oh, hell no. After everything you've been through, I was beginning to wonder if you'd ever crumble—even a little."

"I didn't just crumble, I dissolved."

"Did I help put you back together?"

"Yes." She winced as she remembered that fleeting, troublesome thought that had tried to get her attention earlier. Arnette's warning, which Susan had thought so unnecessary. "Rand...we didn't use birth control."

Now it was his turn to tense up. "You're not, um, on anything?"

"I'm breast-feeding. That at least lowers the chances."

"You're probably right. The probability of your conceiving now…" He laughed, but it was almost hysterical. "Jeez, I can't believe it. That's all you need, another baby."

"Let's not worry about it, okay?" She probably should have kept her mouth shut. Now she'd given him something else to worry about.

"You're right. What's done is done, and worrying won't make any difference. But let's not make that mistake next time, okay?"

Susan focused on just one thing: *next time*. Would there be a next time for them? And how long did it take for those dang birth control pills to kick in? She'd start taking them tomorrow.

He hunkered down under the covers, adjusted the pillows.

Poor Rand. He'd only wanted to comfort her, and he'd ended up a potential father.

She felt compelled to say one more thing. "I would never, ever, try to trap you into—"

"Shh. I know you wouldn't. I know you're not that kind of person. Try to get some sleep, okay?"

Oh, Rand. If he knew the truth about her, he would run for the hills. She loved him, and she hoped Gary stayed lost. She wanted Rand to be Penny's father, not Gary. And she wanted Rand to marry her. She wanted to stay in this house and be with him forever.

His mother was right about her—Susan did have designs on Marjorie's baby boy.

Rand was soon breathing deeply and evenly, but Susan slept with one eye open. When she did doze, she awoke every few minutes, leaned over, and checked to see that Penny was okay. How was she going to handle it when Penny got older? When she took swimming lessons? Rode a bicycle around the block for the first time? Went on her first date in a car with a boy?

Why hadn't somebody warned her how tough it was to be a parent?

PENNY WOKE AT TWO. Rand had been around newborns before, but never this close. It was a wonder the human race had survived if this was what it took, night after night for weeks on end, to get one weaned.

Susan obviously was trying not to wake him as she sat up and worked her legs out from under the covers. But it was too late. So instead of trying to get back to sleep, he propped his head against his arm and watched as Susan found her robe and slid into it, then lifted Penny from the bassinet and carried her into the nursery to change her diaper.

A few moments later they returned. Susan got back into bed, lay down on her side facing away from him, and presumably started to nurse, though he couldn't see.

"Why don't you turn this way?" Rand asked.

Susan jumped. "I thought you were asleep."

"Not much chance of that, when you think about it." He leaned up and peered over her arm.

"Hey, what are you doing?" she asked.

"Watching Penny eat."

"No you're not, you're ogling my breasts."

"That too." He stroked one finger down her cheek. "I won't watch if it bothers you."

"No, it doesn't bother me. Don't get too used to them, though—the breasts, I mean. They're quite a bit smaller in their, um, natural state."

"I'm sure they're wonderful."

He scooted down and nestled his head in the curve of her waist, and she draped her arm over him as she nursed. Rand could have lain there forever, just watching. Mothers and babies were so amazing. Why hadn't he gone into obstetrics?

Actually, he knew why. As an intern, he'd quickly realized he didn't have the bedside manner, the "people skills," to be an effective doctor in any of the disciplines that required lots of compassion and sensitivity. Dermatology had seemed safer. After a couple of years, he'd gotten interested in the research side of medicine and had stopped seeing patients altogether. He actually preferred a sterile laboratory, where he could focus for hours in solitude, than the day-to-day business of seeing real, live people.

At the time it had seemed a rational decision. Now it seemed rather sad. All his life he'd wanted solitude. And now, when he was on the verge of having all the privacy a person could possibly want, he was no longer interested. He'd forged a connection with Susan, whether she realized it or not.

Tomorrow, he would call his private investigator

and take him off the case. He did not want Gary found under any circumstances.

PENNY'S WAKEUP SERVICE worked like a charm. Rand was up, dressed, and eating breakfast with Clark in the kitchen by seven o'clock.

"You're going in early today," Clark commented.

"Couldn't sleep."

"Did Penny wake you up?"

"Uh-huh," Rand answered, flipping to the medical news in his *Wall Street Journal*.

"That's funny. She never woke you up before. If I recall our college dorm days, you slept like a rock."

"Yeah, well, not anymore."

Clark stifled a snort of laughter as he took their dishes to the sink.

"What?" Rand demanded.

"Man, did I call it right, or what?"

"What are you talking about?"

"You and Susan."

How the hell did he know? Rand wondered. Was "Had Sex Last Night" tattooed on his forehead?

"My room is right below hers," Clark said. "And, unlike you, I am not a heavy sleeper."

Rand grabbed Clark's arm as he wiped down the breakfast bar. "You say one word to Susan, and I'll stuff your soufflé pan where the sun doesn't shine."

Clark just laughed. "I won't say anything to anybody. But I did call it right. I knew the two of you would be good together. When she told me she was alone and pregnant, I knew she was the perfect woman for you.''

''Why on earth would you think that?'' Rand asked, bewildered.

''Because she needed someone to take care of her, and you're good at that. I figured you'd be so busy worrying about her welfare, you wouldn't have time to freak out about the fact that she's single and beautiful. She'd get to know you before you did something stupid to sabotage the relationship. And I was right.''

Rand should have been furious with Clark for meddling. Instead, he was dumbfounded by Clark's assessment of his prowess with women. He knew he wasn't exactly a ladies' man, but no one had ever told him he was a complete loser when it came to the fairer sex.

''I never deliberately sabotaged a relationship in my life,'' he objected. ''They just…don't work out.''

''Much to your relief. You gonna mess this one up, too?''

''There's nothing to mess up. Susan and I are friends. There's no commitment between us, not even an 'understanding.'''

Clark pulled a face. ''Yeah, you're gonna mess it up.''

He would have argued further, but a whirring sound from the direction of his office distracted him. Power tools. Aw, hell, she was serious about getting back to work.

He laid down the newspaper, slid off his stool, and went to investigate.

In his office, Susan had a piece of lumber lying across two sawhorses, and she was drilling holes in it. Penny was in her wind-up swing in the far corner of the room.

Susan looked up and smiled. She was radiant, more beautiful than he could ever remember. He really didn't want to go to the lab. He wanted to bundle Susan upstairs and ravish her again.

"Hi," she said. "Are you leaving?"

"Yeah. I thought I'd get in early, then come home early and work on the book. That deadline is creeping up on me."

"You mean roaring toward you like a freight train. It's in two weeks."

"You don't have to rub it in. I won't make the deadline. But I at least want to have a partial manuscript to show the committee when I go to them and grovel for another extension."

"Well, I want more than a partial bookshelf in two weeks. So I'm going to have to put in some hours myself—unless you don't want it finished for Alicia's wedding."

"Alicia would be very irritated if the house wasn't in tip-top shape for her extravaganza."

"But won't the noise bother you?"

"I'll manage." Actually, the prospect of working in the same room as Susan, noise or not, was very appealing. He was quickly becoming addicted to the woman.

"Oh, speaking of Alicia's wedding," he said as casually as he dared, "do you need a date?"

She returned her attention to her work, measuring where another hole would go. "I, um, don't believe I'm invited."

"What? Of course you are."

"Rand, it's a very small wedding, and I'm sure Alicia has more important people to invite than her brother's carpenter. And I could find my own date if I wanted one."

Rand crossed his arms. "I was asking you to go as *my* date. Is it really that hard for you to wrap your mind around that?"

Her head jerked up, a stricken look on her face. "Oh, I'm sorry. It's just that last time I thought you were asking me on a date, you weren't."

"When was that?" he asked, confused.

"That night we all went out to dinner and you baby-sat Penny. I didn't want to assume anything just because we, um..."

His frown melted into a smile. He circled behind her and slid his arms around her. "...because we made passionate love?"

"Shh! Do you want the whole world to know?"

"There's just Clark, and he already knows."

She put down her tools and swiveled around to face him. "You told Clark?"

"He told me. His room is directly below yours."

Susan's face turned bright pink. "Oh, great!"

"Are you kidding? He's thrilled. He's been playing matchmaker all along, you know."

"He has?"

"Yes." Now that she was facing him, he took the

opportunity to nuzzle her neck. "So you'll come to the wedding? The next-door-neighbor's nanny will watch all the young children at her house, so Penny's not a problem."

"Rand, I can't. This is Alicia's special day, and I don't want to risk ruining it by causing tension in your family."

"You mean because of my mother? She'll be too busy to worry about us."

"I don't even have an appropriate dress."

"You think too much." He kissed her thoroughly, and though she was stiff and unyielding at first, he eventually got to her. She gradually relaxed, sliding her arms around his neck, meeting his tongue with hers in a sensual dance.

"Mmm, maybe I could be a little late for work," he murmured into her hair."

She immediately extricated herself from his grasp. "Deadlines, remember? I've got work to do, and so do you." She turned and reclaimed her pencil and ruler, then consulted her plans and started her measurements.

The disappointment he felt was keen, far too sharp than was sane. But she dulled it a bit with her parting words. "There's always tonight."

Those words got him through several hours at the lab, during which more than one co-worker asked him why he was so cheerful.

Chapter Twelve

Susan spent her morning alternately reveling in the memory of her and Rand's lovemaking, then forcing herself to put it out of her mind. Making love to her temporary landlord had to be one of the biggest bonehead moves she'd ever made.

Yet she wouldn't trade the experience for anything.

She had no idea what the future held for her and Rand, but at least her worst fears hadn't been realized. He hadn't been cold to her, or ignored her, or told her it was a big mistake. In fact, he'd asked her on a date—there was no mistaking his intent this time. And he'd made it quite clear that he wanted to repeat their lovemaking.

All the more reason she had to move out of here—fast. The closer she got to Rand, the more it felt like what had transpired between her and Gary. And that was to be avoided at all costs. Establishing her independence would fix everything.

At nine o'clock she retrieved yesterday's newspaper and used Rand's office phone to call a number she'd circled there in the classifieds. Yesterday she'd been unsure she wanted to take this step, but today she felt she had no choice.

A young woman answered in a thick Southern drawl.

Susan introduced herself. "I saw your ad for house sharing and I'd like to talk to you about it. You haven't already found someone, have you?"

"Oh, no, hon, I'm still taking calls. You want to come see the place?"

She sounded nice, Susan thought. "Well, first, maybe you'd better tell me how much the rent is. My funds are pretty limited."

The woman, whose name was Patsy, quoted a price that was surprisingly low. "But I'm looking for a woman with children—I need to work out a baby-sitting trade deal so I can keep my part-time job."

"That's perfect," Susan said. "I have a baby. I'm self-employed, which means my hours are flexible. I'm sure we can work something out."

"Great, come on by, then." Patsy gave her the address. Susan dropped everything, packed up Penny, and headed out. The pretty red truck was in the garage with the keys in the ignition, so she took it. She'd already decided she would buy it somehow.

Patsy was really nice, and her four-year-old, Jonathan, seemed sweet and well-behaved. He showed lively curiosity about Penny, but he was very gentle when he touched her hand, then stroked her cheek.

The house, too, was perfect. It was no castle, but Susan would have her own bedroom and bath, plus full use of the living areas and kitchen. Best of all, the garage featured a workshop add-on, which Patsy was willing to throw in for free.

"I could move in the second of December," Susan said. That was the day after Alicia's wedding.

Patsy hesitated. "Well, I do have a few more people to interview."

"Oh, of course, I understand. Here's my—"

"No, wait. December second? That's a couple of weeks?"

"Yes." Susan didn't want to push it any sooner because she would need every day of those two weeks—only eleven days, actually—to finish the bookshelves.

"Shoot, let's call it a deal." They shook hands, and Susan wrote out a check for the deposit.

She felt a little deflated as she drove back to Rand's. Twelve days. Then her time with Rand would be over. Oh, sure, he might actually hire her to do those other jobs they'd talked about—the kitchen renovations, the fireplace mantel, the storage area in the garage. She'd promised him a hefty discount on those jobs in return for the use of his spare bedroom, so she did kind of owe him the work. But she couldn't really count on that. She knew he'd proposed those jobs in the first place so she wouldn't feel like such a useless lump.

She couldn't count on them being together in any other context. Once she was no longer quite so convenient, he might quickly lose interest. If that was the case, she needed to know.

As soon as she put the truck in the garage, she got

right back to work on the bookshelves. She had to get as much done as possible before Rand got home, because her efficiency level dropped dramatically when he hung around.

When Clark called her to lunch, her stomach swooped. She'd forgotten about Clark, about the fact that he knew what had happened last night. How could she face him?

But she had to eat. She also needed to sit down and rest. Her morning's work had exhausted her. Gritting her teeth, she gathered up Penny from her swing, where she'd been remarkably content, and headed for the kitchen.

"Mmm, what smells so good?" she asked brightly.

"Pan-seared tuna steak, garlic mashed potatoes and sautéed baby carrots."

"Gawd, Clark, how can I lose weight when you're cooking for me?"

"You kidding? This is low fat. That's what we're studying at school for the next few weeks."

Susan studied him, searching for signs of a smirk, of a knowing look. But he seemed his usual, friendly self, not acting peculiar in any way. They ate together the same way they always did, chatting about silly things. Finally Susan couldn't stand it any longer.

"All right, I know you know Rand and I slept together."

Clark's fork stopped halfway to his mouth. "Yeah. I got ears. And I guess we all know where Penny got that awesome set of lungs."

Susan wanted to *die*. "So? Do you think I'm an opportunistic floozy?"

"Susan! No, I don't think you're anything of the kind. In fact, I couldn't be happier about the, um, developments. It's about time you and Rand came to your senses. When it comes time to hire a caterer for your wedding reception, just remember who brought you together."

Susan almost choked. *"Wedding!"*

"You think he's bad husband material? Or maybe he wouldn't be a good father?" Clark raised himself up to his full six-foot-three, daring her to malign his boss and best friend. He was nothing if not loyal.

"No, of course not. He'd be good at whatever he put his mind to. But he won't be putting his mind on marriage."

"You're that sure?"

"Yes! He's told me a zillion times, he's been waiting years for his solitude, his independence. He's earned the right to be a cranky bachelor, and he's going to be one."

"Hmph. Who do you think he's trying to convince, you, or himself?"

"Me. Definitely me. He knows what he wants."

"And how about you? Is your mind on marriage?"

"Clark! Is this any of your business?"

"Is it?" he persisted.

"No! I'm in no position to get seriously involved with anybody. I've got…issues to deal with."

"So, deal with 'em, girl. Read a self-help book, see a shrink, do whatever you have to. But don't let

Rand get away from you. 'Cause when you and your inner child are ready for him, he might not be there for you.''

Susan wasn't sure how this conversation had gotten so out of control. She was sure of only one thing— she loved Rand. Maybe Clark sensed that. But he couldn't possibly understand the complexities working against them, not the least of which was that Penny already had a father. And Susan simply couldn't see Rand playing second-fiddle to Gary when it came to her daughter.

"Can I have a brownie?" Susan asked, indicating the discussion about her personal life was closed.

"Help yourself," Clark said as he cleared the dishes, nodding toward the glass-covered dessert plate on the counter. "But I have one more thing to say, then I'll shut up. Whatever you do, try not to hurt him. He's not as tough as he looks. There's not a man walking this earth who needs someone in his life to love more than Rand Barclay. If he's left completely alone in this house, I'm afraid of what will become of him.''

Their conversation ended there, thank God, because Rand was coming through the garage door. He entered the kitchen with two gallons of paint dangling from each hand.

"Hiya.'' Right in front of Clark he brushed a kiss on Susan's cheek, then Penny's, as he walked past them.

She wanted to sink into the kitchen floor. Did he have to be so blatant?

"Something smells good," he said, obviously full of good cheer. "Is there any left?"

"Of course," Clark said. "What's the paint for?"

Rand set the heavy cans down and rubbed his hands to get the kinks out of them. "For the office. I can't stand the thought of that beautiful bookshelf against those dingy walls. Shouldn't take more than an afternoon to get them painted."

Oh, brother. He obviously hadn't done many home-improvement projects himself, Susan thought, or he would know that painting his office would take *days.*

"What about your book?" she asked.

He shrugged. "I might as well paint while you're hammering and sawing and staining. I can write tonight after you're done."

Susan shared a concerned look with Clark. There was something going on here besides procrastination. It was almost as if Rand was deliberately sabotaging this project.

"Rand," she asked carefully as she slipped off her stool and got herself a brownie, "what will happen if you don't get the book done? If you don't have a partial manuscript to show the powers-that-be when your deadline rolls around?"

A look of uneasiness crossed his face before he quickly schooled his features and shrugged. "I imagine they'll want to know why I haven't gotten more done, and I'll tell them I've been busy, checking more sources, waiting for study results to be published, that sort of thing. Which is the truth, by the way."

"They won't cancel your book contract, will they?"

"That could happen, I suppose."

"And would that make you unhappy?"

"Let's just say my employer would not be giving me a generous year-end bonus. They've extended me every sort of courtesy because of this book. There's no small amount of prestige involved in having one of their staff researchers write the definitive text on dermatology."

"I'm asking about you, Rand. Do you want to write this book, or not?"

"I'd like to know that, too," Clark chimed in as he put a plate on the breakfast bar for Rand.

"Yes," he said, and Susan could see that it did indeed matter to him very much. "I want to write the book. And I will." He walked out of the kitchen, either forgetting lunch or deliberately ignoring it.

"Okay, whatever," Clark muttered as he got out a piece of plastic wrap to put over the plate. "But if he wants something to eat later, he can heat it up his own damn self."

Susan felt like she was walking in a minefield, so she took Penny out in her stroller—another find from Rand's attic—and walked the neighborhood. The weather had warmed up, and she enjoyed looking at all the fine old houses lining the narrow, bumpy streets in Rand's neighborhood.

When she returned to the office to resume work, Rand was there, wearing faded jeans and an old holey sweatshirt, slopping paint on one wall. He attacked the job with abandon, splattering paint everywhere. Figuring this room was no place for a baby, Susan wordlessly moved the playpen to the living room and put Penny down for a nap there.

"You get any paint on my bookcase and you're toast," she warned him when she returned.

"I won't," he said confidently. "I know what I'm doing."

Could have fooled her, but she refrained from commenting.

They worked in companionable silence for a while, though, as predicted, Susan didn't get as much done as she liked. She found herself all too often stalling to stare at Rand, fantasizing about all kinds of improbable things.

Then she remembered her morning's activities. She needed to clue Rand in on her plans. "Oh, I meant to tell you—I found a place to live," she said in a casual tone. "It's nice, and I can afford it. I'm sharing a house with another single mother."

Rand froze. "Where?"

"Over on the west edge of town. It's an older neighborhood with little frame houses and nice trees, and space for my workshop.

"Who's the woman?"

"Patsy Wiger."

"Hmm."

"You don't know her, do you?" Marlena was a small town, but not small enough that everyone knew everyone.

"No. And neither do you. Are you sure it's safe to room with a total stranger?"

"She's very nice, and her little boy is adorable and very well-behaved. We're going to trade off baby-sitting, so it'll work out great for both of us."

"Where's her husband? Or boyfriend, or whatever?"

"He moved out recently, and they're getting divorced. She says it's a friendly divorce, and there are no other men on her radar screen."

"And you believe that? Is she pretty?"

"Why? Do you want me to fix you up?"

"Just answer the question."

He certainly didn't seem very happy about this turn of events. "Patsy is very pretty, and she's about my age."

"When are you leaving?" Rand's voice held little inflection and no emotion. Susan wished she knew what that meant.

"The day after the wedding. Think you can stand me for another two weeks?"

There was a longer than natural pause before Rand answered. "It'll be torture having you around, but I expect we'll survive."

He was kidding, right? Sometimes with Rand, it was hard to tell. His sense of humor was usually kept under wraps, but she had decided that he did have one. It was just rusty from disuse.

Susan forced a laugh. "I'll try not to be too obnoxious, but I can't make too many guarantees about Penny. Oh, speaking of which, I hear her." She escaped for a few minutes to nurse Penny and change her diaper, wondering what was going through Rand's head. Did he want her to leave sooner?

You're getting paranoid, girl. Whether Rand wanted her here or not, she was staying for two more weeks, and there was nothing either of them could do about it.

Before returning to the office, she went into her own room to find a packet of tissues. The paint fumes and sawdust had given her a runny nose. But she stopped in her tracks when she saw a puffy plastic garment bag draped over her bed featuring the name of Marlena's nicest department store. She was almost afraid to touch it, but it drew her like Pandora's box.

Still holding Penny in one arm, she sat on the edge of the bed and reached for the zipper. As she slid it down, a strip of something pastel blue caught her eye. She grabbed the hanger and extracted the most gorgeous, ice-blue beaded dress she'd ever seen.

What was more, it was her size. Or rather, the size she was now, which she refused to claim as her size just yet. She still had ten pounds on her pre-pregnancy self.

Several questions begged an answer—like, where had the dress come from? And who did it belong to? And what the heck was it doing on her bed?

She stuffed the dress back in its plastic cocoon and carried it downstairs, following the sound of banging pots and pans to their source in the kitchen, where Clark evidently hadn't reclaimed his normal good humor. He definitely wasn't accustomed to having people walk away from his cooking.

"Clark?"

He looked up.

"Do you know anything about this dress I found in my room?"

"Oh, yeah, I meant to tell you. It was delivered this morning. I figured it was yours, since it's not exactly Rand's color."

She smiled. "Well, it's not mine. Maybe it's something Alicia ordered when she was still living here, and it's only just now arriving."

"Possible. Maybe Rand knows."

Susan didn't relish going to Rand with the dress. He was acting even more strangely than usual. But she couldn't hide out from him all day. She had a bookcase to finish.

When she stepped into the office, she noted that Rand had finished one wall already, though he'd slopped paint all over the window frames, ceiling and baseboards. She supposed he intended to repaint those, too. And the paint all over *him* would wash off.

"I'll bet you were an enthusiastic finger-painter when you were a child."

Rand looked up and grinned mischievously, calling to mind the little boy he once was. "I never—oh, I see the dress arrived."

"You know something about this?" she asked, hooking the dress's hanger over the door.

He looked decidedly guilty. "You said you didn't

have an appropriate dress for the wedding. Now you do.''

''You…you bought this for *me?*''

''Yeah. Why don't you try it on and see if it fits?''

''How did you even know what size to buy?'' She heard the shrill note in her own voice and cautioned herself to take a deep breath.

''I looked in your closet. Did I do something wrong?''

''Oh, Rand…''

He came down off his stepladder. ''You don't like it?''

''It's a beautiful dress. You have wonderful taste.''

He gave a halfhearted smile. ''The lady at the store helped me out. I told her I wanted something that would look good with black hair and blue eyes.''

''It's not black, really. It's dark brown.'' And what, exactly, did that matter? He was making this really hard. ''Rand, I can't accept this.''

''Why not?''

She took a deep breath. ''Because when a man buys expensive clothing for a woman who isn't his wife, she's usually his mistress. Not just his lover,'' she clarified. ''His kept woman. I'm already living in your house. How will it look when I parade around in designer clothes I couldn't possibly afford?''

''You're telling me you've never let a man buy you clothes before? What about Gary?''

''That was different. Oh, all right, it wasn't that different. He did buy me a few things, but I always felt funny about it. Which is exactly why I'm speaking up now. I did everything wrong with Gary. I *was* his kept woman, more like a pet than a true partner, a possession with no life of my own apart from him. Which meant that when he left, I was nothing—I wasn't even the person I'd been before I met him. I won't do that again. I won't lose myself again.''

"It's just one dress. And it wasn't that expensive."

"I saw the label. You can't touch a Lawrence Raven dress for under five hundred dollars."

He didn't deny her appraisal. "You're being old-fashioned. Who's going to know how much your dress cost and where it came from, anyway?"

"Only every woman in the room. Including your mother. It would offend her sensibilities. It's not right."

He sighed. "I'll send it back, then. Would it offend your sensibilities if I bought you a less expensive dress? We can go to any store you want."

Oh, God, she'd really offended him. He'd been trying to do something nice—again—and she'd shown herself to be an ungrateful wretch.

"Is it that important to you that I attend the wedding?"

"Well, I have to bring a date—family orders. And I can't think of anyone I'd rather spend three boring hours with than you. Um, wait, that didn't come out exactly right."

"That's okay, I know what you meant." She sat down on Rand's desk chair and swiveled it back and forth, to placate Penny, who was fussing slightly. "Okay, here's the deal. I have a dress that I can make do—if I lose another couple of pounds between now and the wedding.'' *And if she let out the seams and wore a corset and held her breath.* "But I want to talk to your mother first.''

The smile he'd been about to show her faded almost before it started. "Talk to her about what?''

"I just want her to get to know me better, and to reassure her that I don't have ulterior motives.''

"I already told her that.''

"Well, maybe she needs to hear it from the horse's mouth. And if she agrees that she can tolerate me at her daughter's wedding, I'll go. Otherwise, I just can't—even though I'm honored you asked me. Alicia's wedding should be perfect, and I refuse to mar it with ill feelings.''

He sat on the middle step of his ladder—no, *her* ladder, only now it was covered with paint—and stretched his arms above his head. "I don't need her approval, you know. I can see whoever I want.''

"Yes, but do you really want her staring daggers at you throughout Alicia's wedding? Wouldn't it be nicer if we all got along?''

Rand scratched his head, getting more paint in his hair. "If you really want to do this, I'll go with you to talk to my mother.''

"I think I should go alone. That way, she can be frank.''

"That's what I'm afraid of.''

"She doesn't scare me. Not much scares me since I became a mother. Parenthood puts things into perspective. So long as my offspring isn't threatened, I can handle anything."

"Then better leave Penny with a sitter. My mother eats small children for breakfast."

"I can win her over."

"You and what army?" He softened the comment with a smile just for her and held out his arms. "What are you doing all the way over there, anyway?" When she didn't immediately leap into his arms, he stood and advanced toward her slowly.

She jumped out of the chair and backed toward the door. "Oh, no, you don't. Have you looked in a mirror lately?"

"You don't think I'm handsome?" He waggled his eyebrows.

All at once Penny made a funny noise. It was something Susan had never heard before. Supersensitive to every nuance of Penny's behavior since the choking scare, she immediately halted the game. "Did you hear that?"

"Yeah." Rand bent to peer into Penny's face.

"I think she just laughed."

"That's impossible," Rand declared. "Babies this young don't laugh. She probably just has gas."

Susan didn't argue, but she knew she was right. Penny wore an unmistakable smile as she gazed adoringly at Rand. Clearly she was bonding with the man she equated with her father.

Chapter Thirteen

For some reason, things started going more smoothly after Susan's chat with Rand about the dress. He sent the dress and the shoes back to the store without another word, and she went to work letting out the seams of a forest-green raw-silk dress she'd bought years ago for a Christmas party given by one of her father's wealthier clients. It would do for a winter wedding.

They managed to work compatibly in the same room, and their conversation became easier, less guarded, though Susan was careful not to bring up the subject of Rand's book deadline anymore. Rand finished painting the walls, then scraped and repainted the woodwork. Susan thought the wood trim ought to be stripped and stained to match the bookshelves, but there was no way to get that done before the wedding, so she kept still about it.

And every night, they made love. Rand usually came to her room, but a couple of times he'd coaxed her into the master bedroom, with its king-size bed. The bathroom, though—that was what convinced her to come back after the first time. It featured a huge shower with his-and-hers showerheads, and a Jacuzzi tub, too. Rand did unspeakably wonderful things to her in both bathing venues.

It was when they were lying together in the whirlpool tub late one night when Rand asked casually, "Why don't you move all your things into my room?"

The question shouldn't have put her on her guard, but it did—perhaps because Gary had leveled just such a question at her shortly after they'd met, and she'd jumped at the chance. Every cell in her body clamored for her to make the same decision this time. Here was a wonderful man wanting to share his life with you—go for it!

But alarm bells screamed in her head at the same time. It wasn't right for her to just take what he was willing to offer. She'd made a vow not to simply allow her life to happen. She was in control now, and jumping into decisions that offered instant gratification was downright foolish.

"I'll be moving out in a few days," she said. "It would be silly to move all my things twice."

He backpedaled immediately. "I meant just some of your things, for convenience's sake."

"There's no place to put Penny," she argued, despite the fact that Rand had set up a baby monitor for those times she spent in his room, so she could hear if Penny made the slightest peep. "Please, Rand, leaving your home is going to be tough enough as it is.

I'm ashamed at how accustomed I've become to living in the lap of luxury. Don't make it any harder.''

She attempted to inject a note of humor into her plea, but underlying it was a thread of desperation. She was so tempted to stay. The worst part about it was, she knew she could. Rand wouldn't ask her to leave, even if he wanted her to.

He took some time to digest what she'd said. The silence seemed to stretch an unnaturally long time before Rand spoke again. "What if you never find him?''

She didn't have to ask who "him" was, or to even question the seeming leap in the topic of their conversation. The problem of Gary was never far from her thoughts. "I won't put my life on hold forever.''

"Then for how long?" he pressed.

"I can't answer that. Till I've done everything I can, I guess.''

"And are you doing everything now?''

"I've sent letters or made phone calls to everyone I can think of who knew Gary. Replies are trickling in, some people are generating new leads for me.'' She didn't add that over the past couple of weeks she hadn't lifted a finger, not even when a former neighbor of Gary's gave her the name and possible hometown of a cousin.

In fact, the three of them—Susan, Rand and Penny—behaved much like a family these days. They'd started throwing their laundry together, and pitching in to shop and cook on Clark's days off. Apparently they looked like a family, too, as evidenced by an embarrassing incident at the mall when an elderly woman stopped them to admire Penny, then declared she had her father's eyes.

Their transformation from an employer-employee relationship to something far more domestic and cozy had been easier than falling off a log—which was a bit intimidating when Susan stopped to think about it. When she moved into her own place, would it be like getting divorced? She worried about the negative impact the move might have on Penny. Even though the baby was far too young to know what was going on, the change in routine might upset her—new smells, new sights, new people around—and some of the ones she was used to *not* around.

RAND FELT GUILTY AS HELL for not mentioning to Susan his efforts to locate Gary. He told himself he simply didn't want to get her hopes up, but something about his hiring a private investigator felt nefarious, and he wasn't sure she would approve. She was so touchy whenever he tried to do something for her or give her something. He never knew when she was going to be sweetly grateful or prickly with indignation.

For now, though, he put his worries aside, as more urgent matters called—namely, the upcoming Thanksgiving festivities. His mother had insisted everyone come to her condo for the holiday dinner this year. Her invitation had pointedly included Clark and Dierdre—he suspected she would put Clark's culinary expertise to good use. But she hadn't mentioned Susan.

What was he supposed to do, leave her home by herself?

"I'll be bringing Susan," he said, telling rather than asking. As far as he knew, Susan had yet to confront Marjorie about the wedding.

A telling silence followed his announcement. Then, finally, a long-suffering sigh. "Really, Rand, I'm sure she has family of her own she would like to spend the holiday with."

"No, she has no family. If she and Penny don't eat with us, they'll spend Thanksgiving alone." Rand was sure this would work. Marjorie liked to manipulate things her way, but she wasn't completely hard-hearted.

"Oh, all right, bring your little carpenter. But I thought just once we might enjoy a holiday without a screaming baby."

"Penny hardly ever screams." As long as someone kept her moving. "Thanks, Mom."

He told Susan the night before Thanksgiving, so she wouldn't have much time to weasel out of it. Predictably, she still tried.

"I need to work on the bookshelves." That was her first attempt.

"Nonsense. They're all but done."

"I don't have anything to—"

"We go casual. Jeans and a sweater are just fine."

"It's a family holiday, and I don't think I should intrude," she said, getting to the crux of the matter.

"But you'll have a chance to talk to my mother about coming to the wedding. You did say you would do that. Besides, Clark and Dierdre will be there, so it's not strictly family."

"But—"

"I'd like you to go."

That was one argument she simply couldn't refute. "All right. But if it ends up a disaster, don't blame me."

THANKSGIVING DAY DAWNED clear and crisp with a definite nip in the air. Susan got up early—as if she had any choice. Leaving Rand to snooze, she tended to Penny, then went to the kitchen to see what Clark was up to. It occurred to her she should bring some sort of contribution to today's meal.

She found Clark already up and laboring over some fancy pastry concoction, which he informed her would be peach-raspberry cobbler.

"I want to make something," she declared. "Would a pecan pie be welcome?" She didn't want to step on anybody's toes if pecan pie was some family member's specialty.

"Sounds good."

"If I put Penny in her swing, could you watch her for fifteen minutes while I run to the store?"

"Fifteen minutes? On Thanksgiving? You're dreaming. Besides, we probably have everything you need here."

Sure enough, there was a huge bag of shelled pecans in the freezer. Susan usually used a frozen pie crust, but Clark wouldn't have such a thing in his kitchen, so he helped her make one from scratch. The rest of the ingredients could be found in any well-stocked kitchen, which of course Clark had.

When Rand finally appeared, looking sleepy and relaxed, she was just taking her masterpiece out of the oven.

"Mmm, I thought I smelled something good." As soon as she'd put the pie on a cooling rack, he pulled her to him for a kiss. She'd long since gotten over being embarrassed by his public displays of affection. She'd even gotten used to him holding her hand or sliding an arm around her shoulders when his sisters or Clark were around.

She kissed him back. "You won't be mushy like this around your mother, will you?"

"Why shouldn't I be? She knows we're more than friends. You can bet my sisters have told her."

Susan groaned. "Then by all means, let's throw it in her face. I'll sit on your lap and then we'll feed each other during dinner, how about that?"

He flashed her an indulgent smile. "Sounds like fun. But you do have a point. I'll try to control myself, okay?"

Marjorie had decreed that dinner would be served at one o'clock so as not to interfere with some bowl game the menfolk were keen to watch. So Susan, Rand and Clark piled into Rand's Bronco at eleven-thirty, picked up Dierdre—who came complete with a huge glass bowl of colorful fruit salad—and they arrived at Teal Lake Villas, Marjorie's retirement village, by noon.

"Wow, this is impressive," Susan commented as they were waved through a guarded gate. Teal Lake Villas was a town unto itself, incorporated just north of Marlena. "I knew this place was here, but I've never seen it."

Posh didn't even begin to describe the area. Glass-and-sandstone houses peeked in and out among the lush greenery as they passed golf courses, lakes, private restaurants, and tennis courts, and streets with names like White Swan Bay Road and Palm Frond Drive.

"This is a *retirement* community?" she couldn't help asking.

"The newest and nicest in South Carolina," Rand said. "Mom didn't want to move here at first, but as soon as she started meeting people and getting involved with the activities, she loved it."

"Wow," Dierdre said. "I can't wait till I retire."

"Not unless you're planning to make a few million bucks first," Clark added.

Susan couldn't help but wonder what had prompted Marjorie to move here in the first place if she hadn't wanted to. "Did your mom live with you before this?" she asked Rand casually.

Clark answered. "Yeah, and she liked to drive us all—"

Dierdre elbowed him. "She was nice enough to invite us, so don't be saying bad things about her."

Rand just laughed. "See, Susan? You're not the only one she's terrorized."

Susan was hardly comforted. Though it was nice Marjorie was happy here, Rand had evicted his own mother when she'd wanted to stay. Obviously he was pretty serious about this solitude business. A wave of guilt washed over her as she once again acknowledged what a kink she'd put in his plans.

Rand turned his car down Woodland Drive and pulled into a driveway. Several cars were already here. On closer inspection, the beautiful, contemporary house was actually a triplex, but it was so cleverly designed that it didn't look or feel the slightest bit like "multifamily."

The front door of Marjorie's unit opened before they'd even climbed out of the car and Marjorie herself emerged, wearing an apron over a perfectly pressed pants suit, smiling broadly at her son. Rand greeted her with a hug and a kiss on the cheek.

"Why are you always the last one here?" she scolded gently. "Clark, Dierdre, I'm so glad you could come. What's that you have, Dierdre?"

"It's ambrosia," Dierdre replied. "It's the only Thanksgiving thing I know how to make. I'm afraid Clark will be the cook in our family. He brought something fancier."

"Susan baked a pecan pie," Clark said helpfully.

Marjorie's smile faded slightly. "Oh, thank you, dear, very thoughtful. Come inside, everyone."

Rand rolled his eyes and whispered to Susan just

before they went inside, "You don't have to talk to her if you don't want to. About the wedding, I mean."

Susan was tempted to abandon her plans. The woman was a tough case. But Rand wanted her to come to the darn wedding, so for him, she would face the lioness in her den.

The moment they stepped inside they were enveloped by what seemed like a dozen little arms as Rand's nieces and nephews greeted them with shouts of "Come see my new game!" and "Read me a story, Unca Rand."

In reality there were only five children—six, counting Penny—but the roar was deafening. And Susan loved it. Bonnie snatched Penny away the moment she got the chance, so Susan focused on the other kids. She watched a doll-diapering demonstration, put a piece into a jigsaw puzzle that one of Betty's girls was working on, pretended to be scared when Shane jumped out at her wearing his fraying Halloween mask.

Having delayed as long as she dared, she went into the kitchen. "Is there something I can do to help, Mrs. Barclay?"

"No, dear, I think we have everything under control."

The kitchen was roomy and ultra-modern, but Betty and Alicia were already helping.

"Speak for yourself," Alicia said. "Susan, are you any good at carving radish roses? These I've done don't resemble flowers in the slightest."

Grateful for Alicia's gesture, Susan tried her hand

at radish carving. The results wouldn't win any beauty contests, but she and Alicia had a good laugh while they worked, enduring diamond-hard glances from Marjorie.

There was no way Susan would get any time with Marjorie alone, she realized. Not before dinner, anyway. The pace was too hectic and there were too many people around.

The dinner was predictably delicious, though Susan resisted the temptation to stuff herself with all the goodies. She kept thinking about the green dress she had to fit into in a few days, which effectively stifled her appetite.

She sat as far away from Marjorie as possible and kept a low profile. Marjorie pretty much ignored her, which was fine with Susan. Maybe, if she just stayed out of Marjorie's way at the wedding...

But after dinner, a golden opportunity presented itself. Susan found herself alone in the kitchen with Marjorie and a mountain of dishes. She dived in and started scrubbing the turkey roaster. Surely Marjorie would give her brownie points for tackling the nastiest job.

Marjorie didn't say a word. It was almost as if Susan were invisible.

Susan wasn't going to let Marjorie get away with that. "The turkey was wonderful. For some reason, whenever I cook a turkey, it comes out dry."

"You have to buy the self-basting kind," Marjorie said, as if any idiot ought to know *that*.

"Oh. Maybe that's my problem." She paused.

"Your house is beautiful. How long have you lived here?"

"About six months."

So much for that conversational gambit. She tried one more time. "The kids sure are having a good time. It's nice when all the family lives close enough that you can get together often."

"How would you know? I understand you don't have a family, or at least that's what you've told Rand."

Whoa! The gloves sure came off in a hurry. Recovering from the momentary shock of Marjorie's rude comment, Susan reminded herself what the objective was here—reassure Marjorie that she wasn't a she-devil out to drain Rand's bank accounts and alienate his affections.

"I used to have a family," she said quietly. "But my cousins lived far away, so we only got to see each other occasionally. And my parents have both passed away."

Marjorie slammed a drawer as she put away some pot holders.

Susan decided she better make her point. "Is there some personal reason you despise me, or is it just on principle?"

Marjorie stiffened, then turned, her mouth twisted with bitterness. "Do you have to ask? You show up on my son's doorstep without a nickel to your name. And before anybody can turn around you've moved in with him. You're eating his food, he's paying your medical bills, buying you cars and God knows what else, and for some reason he's besotted with you. Well, your Little Orphan Annie routine doesn't hold any sway with me. I know your kind.''

Susan put the roaster in the sink drainer and turned off the faucet, then wiped her hands. ''And what kind is that?''

''You're a scheming little opportunist, that's what kind you are.''

Susan's skin prickled with the heat of anger, and her eyes burned with unshed tears. She'd told Rand she could handle whatever Marjorie dished out, but she hadn't been prepared for such a vicious attack.

''So you don't like me because I'm poor, and because I've allowed your son to help me out of a bad situation.''

''I don't have anything against poverty. I've been dirt poor most of my life. But nobody helped me when I had hungry babies and no roof over my head. No white knights came charging out of the clouds to rescue me. I had to take care of everything myself. I made stupid mistakes with my life, but I paid for them.''

Susan just stared, too shocked to utter a word. Marjorie had been poor?

''I see I've surprised you. I guess Rand has never mentioned how he grew up.''

Mutely, Susan shook her head.

''He grew up hungry—and without a father. No rich doctors came along to fix our lives.''

Susan struggled to assimilate this new information. Rand was not from old money. He'd once struggled, just as she was now. Suddenly the idea of her and Rand being a couple didn't seem so absurd.

As for Marjorie, though it seemed ridiculous on the surface that she would take an instant dislike to someone in a situation so similar to hers, it was starting to make sense to Susan. Marjorie saw in Susan a part of herself she hated—a destitute, single mother who'd made too many mistakes. She resented the idea that Susan might escape a life of poverty.

"You think I should pay for my mistakes," Susan concluded aloud, no longer angry. "The way you did."

"You don't even see it, do you, girl? Latching onto a man to bail you out of your troubles is no way to go. And I should know."

That was a lesson Susan should have learned by now, too. But she *was* relying on Rand to fix all her problems. Her token efforts at independence were far from convincing.

She recognized the truth in Marjorie's assessment. Could Susan blame the woman for not wanting her son saddled with a…a parasite?

"For what it's worth," Susan said, swallowing back the humiliation that threatened to bring her to tears, "I'm moving out of Rand's house on the Sunday after Alicia's wedding. I've already put a deposit down on a new place."

"You did?" Marjorie's righteous indignation slipped a bit. In fact, she looked a bit confused that the gold digger wasn't behaving true to form.

"So I'll be out of everyone's hair very soon. But

I have one favor to ask you. Rand invited me to Alicia's wedding. I told him I would go, but only if you agreed.''

"Rand asked you to go? As his...escort?"

"Yes."

"I don't see why you're bothering to consult me. Rand does what he wants.''

"Because I don't want to cause more trouble. I owe Rand a lot, and I don't want to repay him by antagonizing his mother.''

Marjorie grabbed a stack of rinsed plates and placed them in the dishwasher. "It's Alicia's wedding. If she wants you there, then I'm sure it's fine.''

Marjorie was hardly offering her blessing, but neither was she threatening to lob cocktail weenies at Susan if she came to the wedding. As permissions went, it was all Susan was likely to get.

RAND THOUGHT THE afternoon went rather well, all things considered. His mother seemed to have warmed up to Susan slightly. She at least smiled and thanked Susan for helping in the kitchen as they were leaving.

Stuffed and OD'd on football, he looked forward to settling into his office for some work.

But that wasn't destined to happen, apparently. Susan wandered into his office just as he opened up the file containing the chapter he'd been working on. He was ashamed at how welcome her interruption was.

"Did you talk to my mother?"

"Yes, as a matter of fact. She's not ready to nominate me for sainthood, but she sort of said it would be okay if I came to the wedding.''

"I told you she'd get over her snit.''

"It's not exactly a snit, Rand. She has some very real concerns, and she understands far more about my situation than I first realized.''

"I see.'' He sighed. "I guess she told you.''

"Just that you used to be poor. I never had any idea. I assumed you came from old money. How come you never mentioned it?'' He'd been pretty reticent about his past, now that she thought about it.

Rand shrugged. "Those aren't times I care to revisit. I never intended for it to be a big secret. In fact, I figured one of my sisters or Clark had mentioned it by now.''

Maybe they had. They'd dropped hints now and again, but Susan hadn't picked up on them—like when Bonnie had mentioned that she'd never flown in an airplane before meeting her husband, and that their mother wasn't big on vacations.

Which reminded Susan... "Tell me about the vacation in the national park.''

Rand smiled. "Oh, that. We got kicked out of our mobile home and lived out of our car for a couple of weeks. Mom drove to the national park and pretended we were on vacation. It fooled the girls, but not me.''

Susan was developing a whole new respect for Marjorie. She'd been strong for her children, even in the face of homelessness. Susan wasn't sure she could have been that resourceful if she'd ended up on the street with Penny.

"Right after Penny was born, and I got mad because you'd paid my hospital bill, you said something about how someone helped you when you needed it. Was it when you were homeless?"

"Yeah. My great-aunt took us in, but she didn't have room for all of us. Clark's mother offered to let me stay with them. I lived with the Bests for most of my junior and senior years of high school. She helped me apply for scholarships and financial aid and student loans—otherwise, I never would have gone to college."

Ruth Best, Clark's mother. Susan remembered her from when she and her father had replaced a termite-damaged staircase in Ruth's house. She was a warm, smiling woman who was always offering them homemade cookies and hot herbal tea.

"Sometimes heaven sends us angels when we most need them," Susan said. She didn't add that Rand was her angel. He already knew. But an angel's help wasn't meant to last forever.

Chapter Fourteen

Rand seemed edgy Friday morning, the day before Alicia's wedding. It wasn't just that the whole house had been turned upside down by Mrs. Jenkins, the wedding planner. It was something else.

The bookshelves were officially finished. They were beautiful, even if Susan did say so herself. She was particularly proud of this job, the most detailed and ambitious project she'd ever done completely by herself. She'd offered to help Rand store his books and papers in the shelves, file drawers and cubbyholes in a final clean-up effort. He'd taken the whole day off from work to get ready for the wedding.

He didn't seem all that pleased with Susan's assistance. He made a halfhearted effort to organize, often stopping to open a book, read something, and make notes on it.

"Rand, we'll never get finished at this rate," Susan gently pointed out. "Let's just get the stuff off the floor. You can organize it later."

"Or maybe I should just pile it in the backyard and make a bonfire out of it."

Then it hit Susan what was wrong. Monday was his deadline! He was supposed to meet with the committee Monday afternoon and hand over his textbook.

"How much do you actually have done?" she asked him point blank.

"Well, it's hard to mark my progress by the physical pages I—"

"Save it for the committee. How much of a manuscript can you hand over Monday afternoon?"

"About...fifteen pages. That includes my bio, the introduction, and a section on adult-onset acne that's actually an article I wrote a couple of years ago. And I have some of chapter seventeen and chapter twenty-three done. The rest is outlined."

"Rand, as someone who cares about you a great deal, I have to ask you this. What the hell is the problem? You've had eons to write this book."

"I don't know!" He dropped the stack of magazines he'd been about to shelve and sat in his office chair with a thunk. "I've never had writer's block before. Sure, I procrastinate. But I always make my deadlines. I've written dozens of articles and teaching curricula, and all those papers for school, a thesis and a dissertation, and never missed a deadline. I don't know what's going on now. But it's pretty much a moot point, since the committee is going to fire me."

"Are you sure?"

"Almost," he said dismally.

"Will it damage your career?"

"It sure as hell won't help any. Medical research is about ninety percent politics."

"Are there steps you can take for damage control?"

"I could offer to turn over all my notes and research to another writer and take a secondary credit of some kind. That might placate the committee and the lab."

"But you wouldn't be happy about it."

"No. But what choice to I have? I blew it. And the worst of it is, I don't understand why."

Susan moved behind him and put her arms around him, pressing her cheek against his. "I don't understand either, but I still…" *I still love you.* She almost said it aloud. But this probably wasn't the best moment for such a revelation. Rand didn't need another emotional burden at the moment. "I mean, just because you're not a famous author doesn't change how I feel about you. You're a terrific person, Rand Barclay."

He reached behind him, grabbed her arm, and guided her around the chair until she was close enough that he could pull her into his lap.

She went readily, never mind that the house was full people, any one of whom could walk in here. Rand needed her.

He simply held her close. "I'm not feeling real terrific right now," he murmured. "But I do have an awesome set of bookshelves."

"They are pretty, aren't they?"

"I'm going to show them off to every single wedding guest tomorrow, and as each person admires your work, I'll shove your business card in their hand.''

"That would be really tacky."

"Well, you better have your cards ready, just in case.''

She didn't have cards. She had called the phone company and requested a private line be installed in her room at Patsy's house, but she didn't even know the number yet.

She sighed at the thought of moving out. But it had to be done. Things couldn't go on like this, in a fuzzy lavender limbo where she and Rand and Penny were pretending to be a family when they weren't. Marjorie had been right about Susan needing to take care of herself. She and Rand could never have a completely healthy relationship if she continued to be his charity case.

Rand made no move to let her go. ''What do you say we go upstairs, and I have my wicked way with you?''

"Rand! Now? The house is full of wedding planners and florists and party supply people, and Clark's going insane in the kitchen and the grocery store is supposed to be delivering stuff and the house cleaning service is coming—''

"And your point?''

The way he ran his fingers up and down her sleeve gave her goosebumps. When he kissed her neck, her whole body suddenly caught fire. It was always that way with them.

"Let's go now," he said, "while Penny's still napping."

Susan looked at her watch. He was right. They had maybe thirty minutes before the baby woke up.

Feeling positively evil, she slipped out of his lap, which had become less comfortable the more she'd wiggled, and took Rand's hand. They scurried out of the office, across the hall, and up the stairs, almost making their escape. Then Alicia called to them from the living room doorway.

"Rand! I need to ask you something."

"Now?" he asked in a strangled voice.

"Will you change the furnace filters? The dust is making Dougy sneeze."

"Ask Clark to do it."

"Are you kidding? He's up to his elbows in phyllo dough."

"And I've got a book deadline on Monday."

"So is your research upstairs, or what?" She gave him a knowing look.

Susan was dying of embarrassment, but the irrepressible Alicia didn't know the meaning of propriety. "Go change the filters, for heaven's sake," Susan said. "And hurry it up."

He gave her a look that could melt cold steel. "Five minutes." He turned and headed back down, and Susan strolled toward her bedroom.

She didn't have much in the way of sexy lingerie, but she made do with what she had—one pink nylon slip. It would pass as provocative, especially with her temporary D cups straining at the thin fabric. She peeled off her clothes and threw them in the closet, smoothed the slip over her body, and studied her reflection in the dresser mirror.

Not half bad. Another five pounds and she'd have it. And if she sucked in, her stomach didn't stick out at all. She pulled the covers back on the bed and assumed a fetching pose.

Rand arrived in something less than five minutes. Must have been the fastest furnace-filter change in history. He froze in the doorway and stared, his face mirroring surprise and pleasure.

"Well, well, well."

"Twenty-five minutes and counting, buster. Better shed those duds. Or do you...need some help?" She sat up and slunk over to where he stood.

"When did you turn into a sex kitten?" he asked, happily allowing her to peel off his sweater.

Susan wasn't sure why she suddenly wanted to seduce rather than the other way around. Maybe she'd finally stopped feeling guilty for making love with Rand. Maybe she'd finally stopped worrying about what Gary would say if he knew, or whether it would impair her chances of creating a family with Penny's biological father.

She could never marry Gary, not now that she knew what it was like to truly love someone, to love every piece of them, their strengths as well as weaknesses, to love not just what they could provide for you, but what you could give them. With Rand she felt whole again. She could never have that with a man who'd never thought of her as anything but a convenient accessory.

If Gary wanted a part in Penny's life, she would make allowances. But she wasn't going to let him back into *her* life. He'd nearly ruined her. Rand had saved her.

She continued to undress Rand with fevered hands, despite his attempts to explore her body through the shimmery pink fabric that covered it. She couldn't be deterred.

His body was gorgeous, like velvet over steel. She'd asked him once how a fuddy-duddy researcher kept so buff, and he confessed to using an on-site gym where he worked. He'd been instrumental in having the mini-health club installed so that he and his staff and co-workers could live a more balanced life. All of them tended to get caught up in their work to the exclusion of other healthy pursuits.

When she'd finally succeeded in getting Rand naked, she pressed her body next to his, deliberately rubbing her hips against his arousal. He groaned as a tremor shook his body.

"Oh, Susan, you have no idea..."

"I have several ideas. Let's go over them one by one." She led him to the bed with its soft, vanilla-scented sheets, and proceeded to do delicious things to his body with her hands and mouth. She even nibbled on one of his toes, sending him into unexpected spasms of delight.

Finally she lay down next to him and kissed his mouth soundly. "I didn't know you were a toe man."

He cupped her full breasts in his hands, rubbing his thumbs over her sensitive nipples. "I'm a breast man. You're a toe woman. That's how it works."

"You told me you were a leg man."

"I'm a Susan man. All parts of you turn me on, even your earlobe." He tongued the body part in question, sending Susan into her own spasms.

"Enough of this. I'll find out what kind of man you are, once and for all." She hiked up her slip, threw one leg over his body and straddled him. He was hard and hot and throbbing for her, and she was more than ready to consummate their frisky little afternoon delight.

But a deeper, more serious mood lay beneath the playful banter. Their time together was drawing to a close. After he entered her, they rocked together with a quiet, intense desperation, and when Susan reached her climax, the tremors radiated through every cell in her body right to the roots of her hair.

He climaxed almost immediately after she did, and she could tell it was special for him, too. She had to put a hand over his mouth when his cries of pleasure threatened to amuse and/or horrify everyone in the house.

There wasn't much time to savor the afterglow. Right on schedule, Penny woke up with a series of loud, cranky sobs. With a quick kiss to Rand's cheek, Susan slid out of bed and went to see about her demanding child.

She changed Penny's diaper, then took her into the bedroom to nurse. Rand, making no move to dress, lounged next to her and watched silently. He did that often when she nursed Penny in the night, and she always wondered what he was thinking.

POOR ALICIA, SUSAN thought as she sipped her coffee Saturday morning. It was pouring down rain the morning of her wedding. Alicia had spent the night at Rand's house, and she sat at the breakfast table picking at her toast and glancing anxiously outside at the horrible weather.

"Stop worrying about it," Rand said.

"I can't help it," Alicia returned. "What if no one comes? What if the minister gets caught in a flash flood? What if the cake gets dropped in a rain puddle?"

"Wedding cakes never taste very good, anyway," Rand quipped.

"Mine will taste fantastic!" Alicia burst into tears so showy that Dougy stopped playing with his Cheerios to stare curiously at his mother.

Susan shot Rand a warning look and slid into the chair next to Alicia's, putting a comforting arm around her. "A little rain isn't going to keep anyone away," she said. "Besides, it'll probably stop soon."

"But what about 'Happy the bride the sun shines on'?"

"You'll be a bride all day, and by this afternoon you'll be in the Bahamas, where of course the sun will be shining. So stop worrying."

"That's true, I guess." Alicia hiccuped.

"Alicia," Rand said, "if you don't stop crying, you'll march down the aisle with a blotchy face."

This produced a new round of wailing. Susan stared daggers at Rand. "You're not helping."

The doorbell rang. "Fine, then, I'll just answer that." Rand got up to get the door.

"It's probably the flowers," Alicia said, her tears suddenly dissipating. "Or the cake."

It was the cake, followed shortly by the flowers, and various members of the wedding party, as well as several gifts. Susan ushered the bridesmaids, which included Betty, Bonnie and Alicia's friend Angie, into the office, which had become the official bride's room. The wedding planner arrived to soothe raw nerves and masterfully orchestrate every movement and dance around every crisis. The nanny from next door, along with her mother, came over to collect all toddlers and babies. Finally, Susan went upstairs to dress herself.

The green dress fit like a glove. It had a sheer jacket to cover her bare shoulders, and Susan had to admit she felt smart and stylish, though she probably would never forget that blue beaded dress Rand had wanted her to wear. She might have outshined the bride wearing that.

"Get a grip on your ego, girl," she murmured to herself as she put on mascara. But she realized how very far she'd come from that scared, pregnant woman left to fend for herself in what she perceived as a hostile and unforgiving world. She'd felt used up, worthless and unloved.

The world actually wasn't such a bad place, she'd discovered. And it was filled with caring people. Maybe Rand didn't love her with the same intensity she loved him, but he did care for her. Moving out of his home would be hard. But she'd made the decision, she was sticking to it, and even if she went through some initial misery, she knew she would come out of it okay.

When she went downstairs, Marjorie had arrived—wearing a dress almost identical to Susan's. Susan couldn't have committed a worse faux pas if she'd planned it. She did her best to blend into the background, but Marjorie spotted her as Susan arranged wedding gifts on a table in the entryway.

"Oh, hello, Mrs. Barclay," she managed.

Marjorie gave her an appraising look. "Nice dress."

Susan ventured a smile. "And might I say the same?"

"Alicia told me what a wonderful help you've been to her this morning," Marjorie said carefully.

"She just had a little case of bridal jitters. I didn't do much."

"Well, at any rate, thank you." Marjorie didn't smile, and she didn't even stand close enough to touch, but Susan recognized what a struggle it had been for Rand's mother to say those words.

"You're welcome." Susan breathed a sigh of relief as Marjorie tottered away on her spike heels. The wedding was going to be fine. Rand's mother didn't hate her after all.

Susan looked out the front window and noticed that it had stopped raining. The sun peeked out between the clouds.

She ran to the bride's room and burst in on several half-dressed women. Pale peach satin was draped over every chair; shoes and cosmetics cases and bouquets were on every available surface, including her precious bookcase.

Alicia, at least, had on her tea-length candlelight lace gown, but she was barefoot.

"Alicia, quick, come with me," Susan said breathlessly. "This will only take a second."

She dragged a giggling Alicia out the French doors and onto the patio.

"Hey, it's freezing out here!" Alicia complained just as the sun came out from behind another cloud. "What's the big—oh!" She turned her face up into the beaming sun and grinned. "Excellent."

RAND SWALLOWED A LUMP IN his throat as his baby sister exchanged vows with the man of her dreams. Of all his sisters, Alicia had been the toughest to raise—the little rebel. He'd had high hopes for her when she'd been accepted to Georgia Tech, only to have them dashed when she'd come home after one semester, pregnant and abandoned.

Thank God for John. The moment Alicia had met him, all the lovely, graceful, womanly qualities she'd been hiding had burst to the surface. She'd blossomed like a spring daisy. Now Rand could claim he was done raising her.

He glanced at the woman standing beside him. Susan dabbed at her eyes with a tissue. Speaking of lovely, graceful and womanly, he couldn't remember ever seeing her so beautiful. He'd despaired of ever finding a woman who understood even a fraction of what made him tick, and yet here she was. She found his lame jokes funny sometimes, and she liked hearing about his research. She talked about things that fascinated him—politics and ecology and color theory, and even when she talked about the benefits of this baby formula over that one, she somehow made it interesting.

She could be quiet, too, and after living for so many years with his talkative female family members, he valued quiet over all.

She was perfect. And she was slipping through his fingers.

What was he supposed to do? He'd never done the right thing where women were concerned. He had no instincts for it. Should he just let her have her head? Or should he tell her what his true feelings were? Should he try to compete with Gary even when Gary had the ultimate bargaining chip—Penny's DNA?

Should he lock her in her room?

The wedding ceremony was over quickly. The guests filtered into the dining room, where a buffet table groaned with various delights from Clark's kitchen. Rand made the rounds with the guests, playing the part of the proud big brother, posing for pictures with his family, and, when he could, introducing

Susan to people he knew who owned old houses and had lots of money for carpentry projects.

The reception was just winding down and people were starting to drift out to their cars when the doorbell rang. Rand stood in the entry hall talking to his rather tedious banker, so it was a relief to use the new arrival as an excuse to escape.

Feeling slightly heady from champagne and altogether pleased with how the wedding had turned out, he swung the door open. Standing on the front porch was a tall, broad-shouldered man Rand didn't immediately recognize. About thirty, blond, tanned, good-looking in a soap-opera-actor sort of way, the man was dressed in expensive casual clothes—not exactly wedding apparel.

Here to make a delivery, perhaps? "May I help you?" he asked politely.

Then Rand realized he *did* recognize the visitor. Though the picture Susan had been crying over was small, it undoubtedly depicted the man standing before him. Rand's hand bunched into a fist, and he really had to restrain himself from punching that too-handsome face right in the nose. The only thing that stopped him was that he was unwilling to mar Alicia's wedding with violence.

Gary smiled uncertainly. "I'm looking for Susan Kilgore," he said, confirming his identity. "Do I have the right house?"

Rand was so tempted to say no. He'd known this day would come sooner or later, but he'd hoped it would be later. He just hadn't expected Penny's father to be so damn imposing, so immediately...likable.

"She's here," Rand said, refusing to offer Gary more than an ounce of civility. "We're in the midst of a wedding, but if you come with me, I'll try to find her." He escorted Gary to his office, which was the only place he could think of that might afford Susan and Gary privacy. He sure as hell wasn't letting the jerk upstairs near any bedrooms.

He found Susan refilling the punch bowl. "I need you to come with me," he said, ultra serious, not meeting her smile with one of his own.

She gave him a curious look, then set down the glass pitcher on the sideboard and followed him. "Is something wrong?"

Hell, yes. "Not exactly. I have someone here you need to talk to."

"You know, I'm going to have to start paying you a commission. Two of the people you introduced me to want to talk to me about home-improvement projects."

"I don't think this one needs any carpentry." Rand led Susan to his office and opened the door. She stepped inside and inhaled sharply as she saw who was sitting in one of the club chairs.

"Gary? How...how did..."

Rand resisted the urge to stay and watch the reunion. He stepped back into the hallway. "I'll leave you two alone." Walking away from that room was one of the hardest things he'd ever done in his life.

Chapter Fifteen

All Susan's blood drained straight to her feet. Gary? *Now?* She'd visualized her reunion with Gary a hundred different ways, but she'd certainly never thought he would just show up.

He stood up. "God, Susan, you look great."

"Thank you," she said automatically, not at all moved by the compliment. Weird, because she used to melt when he noticed anything about her. "What are you doing here?"

"How can you even ask me that? I was summoned."

"But how did you know where to find me?"

"Your private investigator gave me the address. Why are you standing all the way over there?"

Susan's head spun. "My *what?*"

"That guy you hired. I have no idea how you were able to pay the fee of a guy like that, but he did a good job. Didn't he tell you he'd found me?"

"But I never..."

"Well, hell, it doesn't matter now, does it? I'm here." His voice softened. "I've missed you."

"I missed you, too, Gary," she said with all honesty. But she hadn't missed him lately. The truth was, she hadn't given him a second thought in weeks, except to acknowledge her vague uneasiness that at some point their paths would cross again and she would have to come clean about Penny.

She just hadn't imagined it would happen so soon.

As her head gradually cleared, she realized who was responsible for this reunion. Rand. He was the only person who could have possibly hired a private investigator to track down Gary. The implications were staggering. He must have wanted to unload her pretty bad.

Rand had probably hired the P.I. weeks ago, shortly after she'd come here to live. Now his investment had paid off. He could stop worrying about Susan. Someone else could take over responsibility for her.

Except that she'd already arranged to take over her own life. And the thought of turning herself over to Gary—even if he wanted her—was hideously distasteful. How would he deal with a partner who was no longer needy, no longer hanging on his every word, no longer living her life only to please him?

"What are you doing in this place, anyway?" Gary asked. "Do you work here?"

"Yes, as a matter of fact. Look behind you."

Gary turned toward the bookcases. "What?"

"The bookcases. I built them."

"Oh. Nice."

He turned back. "I'm really happy to see you, Susan. I know the way I cut out on you was kind of cowardly—''

"Kind of?'' Her voice took on a sharp edge.

"I just didn't know what to do. I'd accepted the job in Malaysia—''

"Malaysia!'' No wonder she hadn't been able to find him on her own.

"Yeah. But I couldn't bring you with me. I knew you couldn't handle living in some jungle with no comforts. But I didn't know how to tell you I was leaving, either.''

"Obviously.''

"I thought a clean break would be best. I mean, face it, Susan, you would have begged me not to go. And I don't think I could have taken it.''

There was some truth to what Gary said. She could just imagine now how she would have acted—a clinging vine to the end. She probably would have offered to move to the jungle with him, if that was what it took.

"And I did leave you some money.''

"For which I was very grateful, after I got over being mad.'' At least he'd shown some consideration.

"Then you're not still mad? You understand?''

"I'm not still mad,'' she agreed, amazed that it was so. "I'm sure that I was something of a challenge to live with, and you did what you had to at the time. I'm grateful for the time we had. You sort of held me together at a time in my life when I was falling apart.''

"Yeah, it wasn't all bad.'' His moss-green eyes

appraised her. "You've put on some weight—in the right places, I mean."

Susan swallowed, her mouth suddenly dry. "Um, yeah." She had to tell him. But the words were incredibly difficult. If only she knew how he would react.

Someone tapped on the door, and it opened a fraction. "Ms. Kilgore? Are you in there?"

Susan recognized the voice of the nanny from next door who was caring for Penny. Her heart gave a desperate flutter. "Yes? Is something wrong?"

"Oh, no, it's just that Penny's hungry and you didn't give me a bottle for her. If you'll tell me where it is, I'll take care of it."

Susan glanced uneasily at Gary, who just stared, not quite comprehending the conversation.

"There's no formula—I'm still breast-feeding," Susan said, loudly and clearly enough for Gary to hear. "Where is she?"

"Oh, she's still next door with Mama. You want I should bring her over?"

"I'll come get her. In just a minute."

The nanny took the hint and closed the door. Susan returned her attention to Gary, who now understood the implications all too well.

"You have a baby?"

She nodded. "Your baby, Gary. I was going to tell you the night you left."

He shook his head violently. "That's not possible. We used—"

"We used birth control methods that aren't a hundred percent reliable."

"So this is the urgent business you dragged me out of the jungle for?"

She nodded. Oh, God, was he unhappy.

"Well, I don't buy it," he stated flatly.

Susan was flabbergasted. "You don't believe me?"

"I believe you had a kid. I just don't think it's mine."

"Whose else would it be?" she exploded.

"For starters, how about the guy who lives here, the guy who answered the door? Or am I supposed to believe you're shacking up with him for completely innocent reasons? I mean, come on, Susan. Bookshelves? You don't live with people to build bookshelves."

He had a point. "No, my living here isn't completely innocent," she admitted. "I met Rand a week before Penny was born. But that has nothing to do with the fact that you're the father of my baby. I thought you should know."

"Yeah, so you can trap me into marrying you."

Susan felt sick to her stomach. She'd known Gary had a few character flaws, but she hadn't pegged him for an ultimate, bottom-feeding, slime-sucking jerk. "I have not the slightest interest in marrying you. Furthermore, I'd really like to never see you again. But there is the matter of Penny."

"Penny?"

"Your daughter! Don't you even want to see her? Aren't you curious?"

"If you think the sight of some scrawny, squalling kid is going to make me go all mushy, think again. This little ploy isn't going to work. You'll be hearing from my lawyer."

He edged around her, never turning his back to her as if he were afraid. Then he backed out the door.

Susan wanted to collapse into the nearest chair, her body weak with anger mixed with relief. How could any decent human being turn his back on his own child? And yet, she was glad he wanted no part of Penny. That would simplify her life immensely.

She hoped the lawyer did call, and soon. She would talk to him about drawing up papers to sever Gary's parental rights.

But right now, she had a hungry baby to tend to. She exited through the French doors and made her way next door.

ALICIA AND JOHN RAN OUT the front door under an assault of birdseed, waving and laughing as they gained the shelter of their car. And Rand still couldn't find Susan.

Or Gary.

He could reach only one inescapable conclusion: They'd left together. And it was all his fault. If he hadn't hired the private investigator, she might never have been reunited with Gary. Or, at least, when he'd finally showed up, Rand would have had a firmer hold on Susan's emotions. As it stood, their relationship had simply been too fragile to withstand a reunion with the man she'd spent so many nights longing for.

He wanted to be happy for her. She was getting what she'd wanted all along—a real family for Penny. Gary hadn't seemed that bad. He had, after all, traveled thousands of miles to see Susan. He must have some feelings for her. He must have cared for her a lot at one time, and maybe the binding force of a child they shared would reawaken those feelings between them, cement them, give them a solid foundation.

The fact of the matter, however, was that Rand was so angry he wanted to punch a hole through the wall.

How could a man of his supposed intelligence and education mismanage his life so badly? Over the years he'd watched his sisters make all kinds of mistakes—school mistakes, career mistakes, relationship mistakes. All the while he'd sat above them, gently correcting their missteps, feeling superior that he had a handle on *his* life. He knew where he was going, what he was doing.

And he'd also naively thought that when he actually met a woman he was interested in having a committed relationship with, he would know what to do.

Well, he hadn't had a clue, and he'd blown it.

He should have told her point-blank he didn't want her to leave, ever. He should have bought her the biggest diamond ring he could find and welded it onto her third finger. He should have gotten down on his knees, told her that he loved her, and asked her to be his wife.

Instead, his fears and insecurities had caused him to play it safe. And look where safe had gotten him. He didn't even want to *think* about the shambles he was making of his career. After this fiasco with the textbook, he would never again get the nod for such a plum project. Hell, he'd be lucky if Inman Labs let him wash test tubes when they found out he'd sabotaged the project.

"Rand?" It was his mother. "You look awful. What in the world is wrong? You don't think Alicia's made a mistake, do you?"

Rand realized he'd been staring after Alicia and John's car, lost in his own world. And if his face had reflected his grim musings, it had probably been pretty frightening.

"No, I think Alicia caught herself a keeper. I'm fine, Mom."

"Then it must be that girl."

"If by 'that girl' you mean Susan, you're right."

"Are you in love with her?"

Rand just nodded.

To his surprise, his mother smiled. "I don't believe I've ever seen you distraught over a female. Not even during the worst of your adolescent angst years."

"Never had a reason to be."

"Until now. She must be pretty special."

"She is. But you don't have to worry about her. She's gone."

"Gone?"

"Her ex-boyfriend showed up. She left with him."

"Well, doesn't that just—wait a minute, then who's that?"

Rand squinted in the direction his mother pointed.

His heart expanded as he recognized Susan walking toward him from the house next door, carrying Penny.

He froze with indecision.

"For heaven's sake, Randall," his mother said, and he knew he was in trouble when she used his full name. "Don't just stand there like a ninny. You want her, go after her."

He didn't hesitate another second. He vaulted over the porch railing and met her halfway. He wanted to throw his arms around both of them, his relief was so keen, but he stopped himself. "You're here."

She stopped and looked at him, obviously startled.

"I mean, I thought you'd left. Where's Gary?"

"You thought I left with Gary?" She drew herself up, indignant.

"Well, when I didn't see either of you around..."

"I was next door nursing Penny." Her voice was carefully modulated, her face devoid of expression. "And Gary didn't stay long." Suddenly her temper burst out. "Rand, how could you have hired a private investigator without even telling me?"

"I thought you wanted to find him."

"I did. I just had no idea how badly *you* wanted to find him."

"Because I thought it would make you happy. At first, I mean. But after a while I realized I didn't want Gary to come back. I tried to call off the P.I. But by that time he was already in Malaysia closing in on Gary, and I couldn't get hold of him."

"It's just as well, I guess," she said.

"I guess. You had unfinished business with him,

and until that was settled there was no way...I mean..."

Tell her, for God's sake. Hadn't he just been wishing he'd had the chance to tell her all the things he felt about her and Penny?

"There was no way you'd be rid of me," she supplied.

"That isn't what I was going to say."

Penny fussed, probably sensing her mother's distress. In an automatic gesture, Rand took Penny from Susan's arms and rocked her. He'd gotten pretty comfortable with her lately, and vice-versa. She settled down right away.

They resumed their walk toward his house. Susan would have gone inside, but he stopped her and nodded toward the porch swing. Everyone else had gone back into the warmth of the house, and this was the only place they might have a moment of privacy.

"So, what did Penny think of her f-father?" Rand had trouble getting that last word out.

"She didn't think anything. She didn't meet him."

Rand just stared at Susan, stunned. "You didn't introduce them?"

"I tried. But Gary accused me of lying about his paternity and lit out of here like a roach runs from Raid. He had no interest in even seeing his daughter, much less...much less..." Susan couldn't finish. Her tears cut off her words.

Rand put his arms around her, cradling the baby between them. He had no words of comfort for her.

How did one console a woman who'd just been handed that kind of rejection by the man she loved?

"I don't...even know...why I'm crying," she said, trying to regain control. "I don't love Gary. I don't care anything about the jerk, and I'm glad he's gone. I hope I never have to see him again. It just makes me so...angry...that anyone would turn their back on their own flesh and blood. And it makes me sad that Penny has to grow up without a father."

"No, she doesn't."

With those three words, the air grew so still around them Rand was sure he would shatter it with his own breath. With those three words, he had just crashed through a barrier that had terrified him for weeks. He'd pushed himself to the edge of the precipice, naked and vulnerable, and leaped off. He had no idea whether he'd land in a soft bed or on jagged rocks.

He realized one thing, though. Now that he'd made the jump, he wasn't half as scared as before.

Susan looked up at him questioningly, her eyes still shiny with tears, her cheeks glistening with moisture. "What did you just say?"

"I said Penny doesn't have to grow up without a father. I'm applying for the job." With every word he spoke, his confidence grew. Maybe he wouldn't say all the right words, but by the time he was done, Susan would understand where he stood.

"I don't want you to move out," he continued. "I love you and I want you to stay and marry me, and let me be Penny's father. And we could have more babies. It's a big house. We could have several."

"But…but that goes against everything you say you want!" she objected. "From the first day I met you, you've been talking about your solitude. Your peace and quiet. Time and space to research and write and keep your own hours and watch what you wanted on TV—"

"And I was completely full of it, okay? All these years—*all these years* I've been *preparing* to live my life. I've been coming up with excuse after excuse for why I'm not going after the things I want. I have responsibilities, sisters to raise, money to make, babies to feed, and always that mythical perfect life was right around the corner.

"It's just like that stupid textbook. I've been *preparing* to write it because the actual prospect of writing an entire textbook for Harvard Medical School was so intimidating that I was afraid I couldn't do it."

"So you never really tried."

"Exactly! If I never actually put words to paper, I never had to face the failure of being unable to finish—or, worse, finishing and having the committee tell me my work wasn't good enough. And I never really tried to live my life, either, because I was afraid I wouldn't get the things I really wanted."

"And what things did you want?" Susan asked.

"The same things every guy does," he admitted quietly. "Somebody in my life who thinks I'm the most important person in the world. A kid I can show how to use a microscope. But deep down I thought maybe I couldn't have those things, so I never tried to get them.

"I was afraid to live because I thought I might fail at living. It's a lot safer to put off your life until some day in the future when you're assured of victory. But that day never comes."

"How about today?" Her eyes, so tragic and tear-filled only moments ago, now shone with an optimistic brilliance that nearly blinded him. "I was afraid, too. I was so ready to believe you didn't want me here that I fell all over myself to make sure you knew how badly I wanted to go."

"We're incredibly stupid."

"You said it."

"So is that a yes? You'll marry me?" Rand wasn't going to let her slither around. He wanted answers. He was going to pin her down to a date and a place.

"You don't mind if I continue with the carpentry?"

"Of course not. I want you to do whatever makes you happy."

"Your mother will think she was right all along—that I *am* a gold digger."

"My mother told me to go after you. And you're running out of objections. Unless...unless you just don't want—"

"Yes, I'll marry you! Whenever, wherever you say."

Rand smiled, relief washing through his body. "Want me to catch the minister? He might still be here."

"I think we have to fill out paperwork first."

Rand didn't want to think or talk about paperwork. He kissed her, still snuggling Penny between them. The baby seemed to like the added security of two warm bodies surrounding hers. She cooed and smiled.

Yes, Penny definitely smiled.

TWO WEEKS LATER, at 5:00 a.m., Susan watched with bleary eyes as the last page of Chapter Nine rolled off Rand's printer. The textbook was far from complete, but he had at least twenty-five percent to show the committee.

He had called the committee head first thing Monday morning and made a full confession as to his lack of productivity. Dr. Kensington was predictably upset, but Rand was able to soothe him with a not-altogether-true promise that much of the book was written, just not polished. He promised to produce the first two hundred pages in two weeks, and the balance of the book at the end of February, if the committee would see clear to extending his deadline one more time.

Dr. Kensington had been on the verge of saying no until Rand had agreed to make a generous donation to the doctor's favorite research project. Bribery, pure and simple.

With a two-week reprieve, Rand hadn't wasted a moment. He'd taken an unscheduled vacation from the lab, then he'd sat down in front of the computer and started writing. The words, sentences and paragraphs seemed to come remarkably easily once he started. His careful preparations were paying off. The information was there; all he had to do was transcribe it into readable form. And Susan's job was to crack the whip.

Susan never left his side. When his fingers cramped from too much typing, she sat down in front of the keyboard and took dictation from him. Clark brought their meals to them in the office. Penny cheered from her swing, and her playpen, and her second crib, which Clark had brought down from the attic. Sometimes she cheered from her papoose position on Rand's back.

Rand got little sleep, but he got the pages written. Susan was amazed by his energy, his excitement.

Susan had been so involved in Rand's book, in fact, that she'd given little thought to their wedding, which was tomorrow. They'd let Clark and Marjorie make all the preparations for their simple, family-only ceremony. The wedding was only a formality, anyway. The day they'd committed their love on the front porch, they'd started living as husband and wife.

She'd worried about disappointing Patsy, and Rand had offered to pay Susan's share of the rent *and* to take care of Patsy's little boy while she worked, but as it turned out, that wasn't necessary. Patsy's husband had come home, they'd agreed to give their marriage another try, and Patsy had been relieved she didn't have to honor Susan's lease.

Gary's lawyer had called, as promised, and Gary had been only too happy to deny all rights and responsibilities where Penny was concerned. With a notarized signature he was off the hook and on a plane back to Malaysia—and out of Susan's and Penny's lives for good.

"You are going to knock 'em dead," Susan said as she stacked the partial manuscript neatly and boxed it up. She would take it to the copy shop while Rand showered and dressed for his meeting with the committee. "I'm not even a medical student, and *I* enjoy reading the book."

"You have to like it. You're almost my wife. What if it's terrible?" he asked with a sudden case of nerves.

She shrugged. "Maybe they won't like it. Maybe they'll fire you. But at least you gave it your best shot. And even if they hold their noses and call for a toxic waste disposal SWAT team to get rid of the manuscript, I'll still love you."

He laughed and hugged her. "Well, thank you for *that* lovely mental image."

She kissed him. "No, thank you. For letting me help, for letting me give something back. You've done so much—"

He hushed her with a finger to her lips. "You give back every time you look at me. Because I see in your eyes what I've always wanted to see, what I never thought I'd see."

Susan didn't doubt it. He and Penny were the most important people in the world, and her love and respect and trust and loyalty probably shined out of her ears as well as her eyes twenty-four hours a day.

But he wasn't the center of her universe, an important distinction for her. She was no one's satellite. It was more like she and Rand were twin suns, spinning around each other.

Twin suns with an adorable little planet named Penny.

"Go take your shower," she said, giving him one final kiss on the nose. "I'll go to the twenty-four/seven copy shop, and I'll bring home some gourmet coffee and éclairs to celebrate."

"We can't claim victory yet."

She flashed him a knowing smile. "Oh, yes, we can. We've won every battle that's truly important."

Three powerful tycoons
don't know what hit 'em in

Just for Kids

a brand-new miniseries by

Mary Anne Wilson

only from

◆ HARLEQUIN®

AMERICAN *Romance*®

They're smart, successful men with heads for
business—not babies. So when they come face-to-face
with tons of tiny tots, only the love of these good
women can show them how to open their hearts....

REGARDING THE TYCOON'S TODDLER...
HAR #891, on sale September 2001

THE C.E.O. & THE SECRET HEIRESS
HAR #895, on sale October 2001

MILLIONAIRE'S CHRISTMAS MIRACLE
HAR #899, on sale November 2001

**Welcome to Just for Kids, a day-care center
where *care* is the most important word of all.**

Available at your favorite retail outlet.

HARLEQUIN®

*M*akes any time special ®

Visit us at www.eHarlequin.com   HARKIDS

WANTED:
Women and babies
WHERE:
Shotgun Ridge, Montana
WHEN:
As soon as possible!

The old folks in Shotgun Ridge, Montana,
aren't satisfied yet. The town's still a little light on
the ladies, and no bachelor is safe! So come on
back for more brand-new stories about the

by
**MINDY
NEFF**
from

HARLEQUIN®

AMERICAN *Romance*®

#898 CHEYENNE'S LADY
November 2001
#902 THE DOCTOR'S INSTANT FAMILY
December 2001
#906 PREACHER'S IN-NAME-ONLY WIFE
January 2002

Available at your favorite retail outlet.

Visit us at www.eHarlequin.com

HARLEQUIN®
Makes any time special®

HARBACH

There's a baby on the way!

HARLEQUIN

AMERICAN *Romance*

is proud to announce the birth of

AMERICAN *Baby*

Unexpected arrivals lead to the sweetest of surprises
in this brand-new promotion celebrating the love
only a baby can bring!

Don't miss any of these heartwarming tales:

SURPRISE, DOC! YOU'RE A DADDY! (HAR #889)
Jacqueline Diamond September 2001

BABY BY THE BOOK (HAR #893)
Kara Lennox October 2001

THE BABY IN THE BACKSEAT (HAR #897)
Mollie Molay November 2001

Available wherever Harlequin books are sold.

HARLEQUIN®
*M*akes any time special ®

Visit us at www.eHarlequin.com   HARBABY

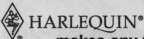

HARLEQUIN®
makes any time special—online...

eHARLEQUIN.com

your romantic
books

- ♥ Shop online! Visit Shop eHarlequin and discover a wide selection of new releases and classic favorites at great discounted prices.

- ♥ Read our daily and weekly Internet exclusive serials, and participate in our interactive novel in the reading room.

- ♥ Ever dreamed of being a writer? Enter your chapter for a chance to become a featured author in our Writing Round Robin novel.

• • • • • •

your romantic
life

- ♥ Check out our feature articles on dating, flirting and other important romance topics and get your daily love dose with tips on how to keep the romance alive every day.

• • • • • • •

your
community

- ♥ Have a Heart-to-Heart with other members about the latest books and meet your favorite authors.

- ♥ Discuss your romantic dilemma in the Tales from the Heart message board.

your romantic
escapes

- ♥ Learn what the stars have in store for you with our daily Passionscopes and weekly Erotiscopes.

- ♥ Get the latest scoop on your favorite royals in Royal Romance.

All this and more available at
www.eHarlequin.com
on Women.com Networks

HINTA1R

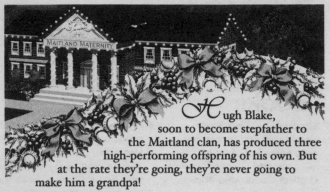

*H*ugh Blake,
soon to become stepfather to
the Maitland clan, has produced three
high-performing offspring of his own. But
at the rate they're going, they're never going to
make him a grandpa!

There's *Suzanne*, a work-obsessed CEO whose Christmas spirit could use a little topping up....

And *Thomas*, a lawyer whose ability to hold on to the woman he loves is evaporating by the minute....

And *Diane*, a teacher so dedicated to her teenage students she hasn't noticed she's put her own life on hold.

But there's a Christmas wake-up call in store
for the Blake siblings. Love *and* Christmas miracles
are in store for all three!

Maitland Maternity
Christmas

A collection from three of Harlequin's favorite authors

Muriel Jensen
Judy Christenberry
&Tina Leonard

Look for it in November 2001.

Visit us at www.eHarlequin.com   PHMMC